Put Out the Light

Put Out the Light

A RED BADGE NOVEL OF SUSPENSE

RAE FOLEY

DODD, MEAD & COMPANY · NEW YORK

Library of Congress Cataloging in Publication Data

————————

    Put out the light.

    (A Red badge novel of suspense)
    I. Title.
PZ3.D426Pu [PS3554.E56] 813'.5'4 76–26512
ISBN 0–396–07352–2

For my dear Ann

Put Out the Light

One

I checked out of the Commodore, refused the services of a bellboy and, shuffling and pushing, managed to get my three large suitcases and small dressing case into Grand Central Station, where I hoisted them into a locker. I had no idea of what the future held beyond the next hour, but at least there was no hotel bill to pay and I was temporarily free of encumbrances. With visions of New York streets being filled with pickpockets, if not with muggers, I gripped my bag tightly under my arm. Aside from the usual woman's paraphernalia it held a billfold containing over a hundred dollars, the most money I had ever carried at one time in my life. It also held a letter addressed to Miss Constance Armstrong and signed in a neat prim hand, "Brendon Fowler."

According to the letterhead Mr. Fowler was a partner in the law firm of Wellington, Fowler and Crisp. In spite of the legal verbiage, which, like a doctor's prescription, seems designed for the obfuscation of the layman, I was aware that it was not a friendly letter. Mr. Brendon Fowler obviously did not approve of his client's action in opening her home to a niece whom she had never seen and of whose existence she had not known until six weeks earlier when I had written to tell her of my mother's death.

That letter had deliberately been framed in a "see what you have done" manner and I had not expected a reply,

1

certainly not the warm response that not only offered me a home and a genuine welcome but implied that my future would be free of financial worries. At the time it had seemed too good to be true, and when it was followed by the lawyer's letter, I knew something was wrong. In accordance with his client's instructions, he suggested that I get in touch with him as soon as I reached New York, as he understood that Mrs. Clifford—he did not commit himself by saying "your aunt"—had invited me to her home. An impulsive and fantastically generous woman, Mrs. Clifford frequently made injudicious decisions, but we could doubtless come to some satisfactory compromise. He remained, very sincerely, Brendon Fowler.

Angry as that letter made me, I'd have accepted my aunt's invitation if she had been Lady Macbeth. In the same mail I had received a letter from my landlord, who wrote regretfully that he could not carry my rent for another month, and a doctor's bill that looked like the national debt.

The law firm of Wellington, Fowler and Crisp, I discovered, was just across Forty-second Street from Grand Central Station. New York was a giant mass pressing on me, as though the great stone towers were leaning over, trying to crush me. The noise of motors, of police whistles, of steel riveters, of trucks, of jostling people speaking many languages, beat against me in a deafening cacophony. In a sudden panic I raced across Forty-second Street against traffic, accompanied by a blare of indignant horns, a policeman's whistle, and a burst of profanity from a taxi driver who had to stand on his brake to avoid hitting me.

I leaped for the curb, my heart racing, more demoralized than when I had started out that morning to keep my appointment with the lawyer who sounded so hostile, so forbidding. Mr. Fowler had requested that I provide proof of identity, as though he expected some impostor to attempt to pass herself off on Aunt Natalie's charity.

The firm was listed on a wall directory that seemed to contain the names of half the inhabitants of New York. I found the proper bank of elevators and the door slid open noiselessly and decanted me into an austere waiting room with a reception desk at which sat an austere middle-aged woman who was talking noiselessly into the telephone. There were half a dozen austere black-leather chairs that were about as inviting as the benches at Grand Central Station. Only one other person was there—a tall, lanky young man, loosely put together, with a lock of fair hair drooping over his forehead, which he constantly shoved back with an impatient gesture. He was flipping the pages of *Forbes* magazine with manifest boredom.

I went up to the receptionist desk where I was surveyed through bifocals. "May I help you?"

"I have an appointment with Mr. Fowler. My name is Armstrong. Constance Armstrong."

The impatient young man looked up alertly and thrust back the lock of hair. The receptionist inclined her head toward those stiff leather chairs. "Have a seat. I will inform Mr. Fowler."

I sat on the edge of my chair, holding my handbag so tightly that my fingers felt cramped. The receptionist spoke quietly into the telephone, and all the time her eyes never left me, though she could hardly have expected me to make off with one of those chairs. Anyhow, judging by the general atmosphere, I'll wager they were screwed down.

"Not unlike being screened by the CIA, is it?" the young man said, grinning and not bothering to lower his voice. "They only do it to undermine your morale," he went on cheerfully.

"That wouldn't be difficult," I admitted.

3

"Just think of them as a pack of cards; faces on one side, nothing but numbers on the other, all assembled by computers."

The receptionist was not amused. She gave him a repressive look and then, as though in rebuke at such frivolity, attacked her typewriter in a burst of furious speed, though the typewriter itself was, of course, noiseless. Unseemly sounds were not tolerated in these precincts.

Another middle-aged woman—the law firm of Wellington, Fowler and Crisp did not run to glamour—came into the room and opened the little gate. "Miss Armstrong? Mr. Fowler can see you now. Will you come this way?"

Apparently I did not rate top treatment. I followed her along a corridor, past an impressive law library, past small cubicles used as conference rooms in which men talked quietly, past doors bearing the names of several junior lawyers and finally a wide oak door with the name MR. FOWLER in gold.

The secretary stood back for me to precede her. "Miss Armstrong," she said in a tone of modest achievement at having delivered me safely.

For a moment I was blinded by the brilliant sun pouring in the windows. After southern California I was not adjusted to the deep blue vividness of an October sky and the glitter of sunlight reflected on thousands of glass and steel buildings. Then I observed the spacious office with its deep carpeting, its beautifully hung maroon drapes, its walls covered with ornately framed portraits of grim men in the high stocks of a century and a half ago and more recent ones in contemporary dress. It was to be hoped that they compensated in ability for what they lacked in charm, and I assumed that they must. This kind of opulence had not grown out of ineptitude.

Last of all I became aware of the man who had risen from behind an impressive desk, risen at the last possible moment for courtesy. He did not come forward to shake hands with me. He was perhaps fifty, beautifully groomed in contrast with the casual and usually sloppy attire of the California men to whom I was accustomed, often jacketless and frequently without neckties. This man would as soon have appeared without his shoes as without his jacket. He was tall and thin, with a narrow, clean-shaven face, gray hair cut very short, and horn-rimmed glasses.

He stood unmoving at his desk, his eyes riveted on me. "Good God!"

Whatever I had expected, it was not a greeting like this. I blinked, partly in sheer astonishment, partly because the light dazzled me and made it difficult for me to see him clearly.

Then, as though there had been no interruption, he came to take my hand for a brief moment, still staring at me with a kind of incredulity and shock.

"Sit down." He indicated the chair beside his desk. It faced squarely into the blinding light, while his own seat, behind the huge desk, had its back turned to the windows.

My timidity and uncertainty were lost in a flare of anger. Whether Mr. Fowler thought me an imposter or, at best, an indigent relation trying to sponge on her rich aunt, I had had it.

"Sorry, but the light hurts my eyes." I moved to a chair some distance from the desk where the folds of heavy drapery shielded me from the glare. At the expression of surprise on his face I thought: One up for me, instinctively aware I was engaged in some sort of contest with this man, but a contest in which, unfortunately, I did not know the rules.

Aware that he was still giving me that long, close inspection, I opened my bag and held out the letter he had written me. "You wanted me to provide proof of my identity. I thought the best thing would be to bring back your letter.

My birth certificate is in a safety deposit box in Beverly Hills, but I have lost the key. You could probably get a copy of the certificate from the Bureau of Vital Statistics in Beverly Hills, where I was born. I haven't anything else."

He took the letter without a glance and dropped it on his desk. "You need no proof of identity," he said in a curious tone. "You carry it with you." Seeing my surprise, he asked, "Didn't your mother tell you that you look exactly as her sister Natalie did at the same age?" The shock was still in his eyes. "It's fantastic."

"My mother rarely mentioned any of her family." I felt the familiar anger lick through my veins. "There was no reason why she should. Her family dropped her from the time she married. Her father disinherited her. Her sister let her starve." I could hear the betraying tremor in my voice.

The lawyer put out his hand with an angular gesture, mutely protesting my vehemence. "Miss Armstrong, surely this bitterness is quite unjustified. The very fact that you are here now—"

"It's a little late, isn't it, for Aunt Natalie to try to make amends?"

His eyes flickered and I knew that he was angry, but he had the advantage. His temper had long been under disciplined control, while mine, Heaven help me, had not. Or perhaps I had brooded too much, stoked a fire that should have been allowed to die.

"I must point out to you that your aunt knew nothing of your mother's circumstances or her whereabouts or even of your existence until she received your letter telling her with needless brutality that your mother had died of neglect. The news came as a great shock to Natalie, who is a sensitive and lovely person. Her first thought was of you. She wrote me, explaining what had happened, and saying that she had urged you to come east at once to live in the house where your mother grew up and which, she felt,

6

belonged by rights to you as much as to her. She is keenly aware of her father's grave injustice in leaving everything to her instead of dividing it between his two daughters.

"In fact," the lawyer picked up a paperweight and stared at it as though he had never seen it before, "she immediately arranged to change her will. Before leaving for Europe on her honeymoon, she drew up a will leaving everything to her husband. Now, in view of her—and apparently your—theory that you have a just claim on her, she has given orders to change her will, dividing her estate equally between you and her husband. If you feel that her action comes too late for your mother, at least you may be assured that Natalie is doing everything in her power to arrange things as a compensation for what your mother suffered; though I must say I fail to see in what way Natalie was to blame for her father's disposal of his own estate. However, with her usual impetuosity she wrote that she had sent you an ample check to take care of any outstanding debts, to provide for your traveling expenses, and enable you to get the kind of wardrobe you would need here, as she feared you were very poor indeed."

His eyes flickered over my beautifully tailored gray flannel slack suit, the impeccable blouse, shoes and handbag. My hair was brushed high off my face, its natural curl disciplined into waves, emphasizing my eyes, which are my best feature. I met his scrutiny without fear. Though I had never had enough money to indulge my taste, I had a flair for clothes and I knew there was no flaw in my grooming. But my pleasure was embittered by the awareness that to Brendon Fowler I was a charity child decked out by Aunt Natalie's benevolence.

Once more the lawyer shook his head in a kind of incredulity. "The resemblance is uncanny. You aren't at all like your mother, but you might be Natalie's daughter."

"Well, I wasn't," I said, and again his eyes flickered.

7

"Before going up to the family house in Alcott, there are a few things you must understand. First, as you are aware, your aunt is deeply and passionately in love with her husband."

"I? How could I possibly know?"

"You haven't read her poems?" This time the lawyer was visibly shaken.

"I didn't even know she wrote poetry."

"Good God!" he said again in that same tone of wonder and shock. "Not even *Prismed Light?* Why, she was awarded the Pulitzer Prize for poetry."

I boiled over. "Aside from the fact there was no money to buy books, there hasn't been much time for reading either. For the past two years I've spent my days typing for a movie studio; my weekends and evenings and a lot of nights were devoted to nursing my dying mother. There wasn't time for poetry; just enough for basic shopping and laundry and cleaning the apartment and later a furnished room, and keeping my clothes washed and pressed and mended so I could go to work."

The lawyer had a judicial and impersonal manner as though he spoke from the bench. "I can see that you have had a difficult time of it and I understand that you have permitted yourself to become bitter—I might say obsessed —about what struck you as unfair treatment. But it is pointless to inveigh against the dead. The injustice, if it was injustice, was not Natalie's work, it was her father's. And," irritation crept into his dry, detached manner, "considering that you are less than enthusiastic about typing, I should think the prospect of a comfortable, not to say luxurious, home for life and a generous income after her death —if she actually signs that new will—would be some cause for gratitude."

One question had tormented me for years. "Why did my grandfather behave as he did to my mother?"

"That was a long time ago."

"And besides, the wench is dead. But it surely concerns me; it has shaped and affected my whole life."

"Can't you let sleeping dogs lie?"

"No, I can't."

"After all, you've heard only your mother's side."

"She never said a word about it."

The lawyer removed his glasses and polished them carefully. "You understand, don't you, Miss Armstrong, that I am taking a risk in confiding in you. If you carry your bitterness and resentment to the point of discussing these matters with Natalie, you could do immeasurable harm. She was an invalid for more than twenty years. This marriage has brought her the first, the only, happiness she has ever known. Are you prepared to destroy it?"

He seemed to be satisfied with what he saw in my face. "Old man Netherfield had a violent temper." He permitted himself a faint smile. "One which, I suspect, you have inherited. He and his wife were incompatible; it wasn't exactly an unhappy marriage, but she was—subdued. Very subdued. It might have been better if she had been the kind to fight back.

"Anyhow your mother was like her mother and Natalie, two years younger, was the family beauty. From the time she was born everyone made a fuss over her, everyone spoiled her and, as a result, Florence was rather overlooked. Until, that is, she made a brilliant debut as a pianist at twenty-two. That took her away from home on her first concert tour where she met your father. I suppose George Armstrong was the handsomest man I ever met in my life. You wouldn't remember that."

"I've seen him in some late, late movies. And, anyhow, it wasn't that long ago."

"Well, he met Florence somewhere, they got acquainted, and he went up to Alcott to visit her. Then he met Natalie.

The next thing I knew Florence had eloped with George. I suppose she married him as soon as she could because Natalie was—well, Florence, to be honest about it, never had an admirer who did not turn to Natalie. No one's fault. Just the irresistible attraction of beauty and that curious sort of other-world quality, a kind of glow she had. So the elopement came as a shock to the whole family."

"In other words, my mother wasn't expected to have anything!"

The lawyer's eyes were hard. "You are a very prejudiced and unjust young woman. Two weeks later, Natalie went swimming on Long Island, went out too far and got a cramp. Her mother, who was a strong swimmer, managed to lift her onto a raft and haul her aboard, and then she collapsed and died of the strain. She had fatty degeneration of the heart and she had been warned of overexertion.

"Natalie strained her back when she was hauled onto the raft, and the shock of her mother's death, for which she blamed herself, plus the back injury, made an invalid of her for years. Her father's death followed her mother's not long afterwards, so she became a recluse, shut away from the world. She had only her poetry and her growing reputation until Jack Clifford appeared on the scene, one of the few admirers whom she had been willing to receive. He remade her world.

"I want her to stay happy, Miss Armstrong. She has it coming to her. If your mother had a disappointing life, Natalie had none at all. She felt—rejected." He looked at me intently and said, "Like you."

I thought honestly: One up for you.

"In all fairness, Miss Armstrong, I must point out that Natalie was not responsible for your mother's unhappy life and her untimely death. I agree that old man Netherfield behaved in an outrageous manner. He managed to blame Florence for everything that happened, including Natalie's back injury and her mother's death. He disinherited her and uttered all the Victorian clichés about never darkening his door again. But Natalie was the victim and not, as you appear to believe, the villain. Nor was she even remotely responsible for the fact that your father, the once famous George Armstrong, landed on Skid Row as an alcoholic."

So there were to be no holds barred.

"For five years," I told him, "I have believed there was something behind my father's ruined career."

"There was. He drank. It's as simple as that."

"He hadn't started drinking and he had lost none of his acting ability when the studios stopped giving him top billing, and then he dropped to second leads, and then smaller and smaller parts. He was fighting an enemy he couldn't see, but I have always believed some rival—"

Fowler laughed gently. "What an unbridled imagination! I suppose you don't know where your father is now."

"Not after he realized he was being blackballed by the studios and he couldn't support us any more. It was too late for my mother to take up her career, so she clerked in a dress shop. One day he went away leaving a note saying he was no good to us, no good to anyone. He loved us too much to be a stumbling block. After that, I saw him occasionally on the street, growing shabbier and shabbier, and once he was staggering. That was the last time."

Fowler reached out a dry, bony hand to silence the telephone. "No, not this afternoon. In fact, cancel everything until next Monday. I won't be back after lunch, Oh, and please find a Mr. Struthers in the waiting room and send him in."

He turned back to me. "I have arranged to drive you up to Connecticut and settle you in your new home this afternoon. As you know, your aunt will be returning tomorrow from that round-the-world honeymoon and she will expect to find you there."

11

"It's strange, isn't it, to think of a middle-aged woman going on a honeymoon."

There was an odd expression on the lawyer's face. "To you—at twenty, isn't it?—that is probably true."

"What is the bridegroom like?"

"An attractive man. Devoted to Natalie. The chief thing is that he has made Natalie a happy woman."

"How will he feel about having a stranger in the house, and particularly one who may share in his wife's estate? That is, if he should survive her."

"Oh, he'll survive her. Bound to," the lawyer said. "He is twelve years younger, you know." As his secretary, with the air of a tugboat successfully bringing an ocean liner into port, announced, "Mr. Struthers," Fowler said, "I meant to tell you that there will be another house guest, one who will also be making an indefinite stay in Alcott."

He got up to shake hands with the tall, rangy young man who had been in the waiting room when I arrived. "Mr. Struthers? Sorry to keep you waiting. This is Mrs. Clifford's niece, Miss Constance Armstrong. Mr. Timothy Struthers is going to Alcott to gather material for a biography of your aunt. If you are ready, we may as well lunch now. There's a convenient restaurant on the roof garden."

"Thank you. That would be very pleasant." Mr. Struthers shook hands with me, a firm, brief handshake. When he shook hands with people, he looked at them as though he really saw them and liked meeting them. I found myself smiling back.

"I thought we'd leave for Alcott immediately after lunch, if that is satisfactory for you." The lawyer's manner made it clear that we had better find it satisfactory. "Where is your luggage?"

"In a locker across the street at the station," Struthers said. "One briefcase, one typewriter, one suitcase. I have to get around a bit, so I've learned to confine myself to basics."

"Good." Fowler looked at me, obviously expecting the worst.

"Mine's at Grand Central too. I checked out of the Commodore this morning because I didn't want to pay another night's rent, and I wasn't sure what the plans were. I have rather a lot: three suitcases and a dressing case. I didn't know—" The words trailed off.

Mr. Fowler stood back to let me precede him, followed by Mr. Struthers. I caught my bag on the door frame and turned to release it, getting a quick glimpse of the lawyer's face. He didn't like the young man any better than he liked me. He acted as though he were watching helplessly while the Trojan horse was being wheeled within the city gates, the enemy within the walls. I wondered if Struthers was aware of the lawyer's antagonism and distrust. Seeing a quirk of amusement at the corners of his mouth, I rather thought he was.

Two

The roof garden restaurant, which apparently catered only to executives and their guests, was run as I had always imagined a fine English club being run—with beautifully appointed, widely separated tables, unobtrusive and deferential service, and generally muted voices, which gave the impression that matters of momentous importance were being discussed. Certainly most of the diners presented a stereotype of men on whose shoulders rested matters of great weight carried with becoming solemnity. The atmosphere was not conducive to gaiety.

Mr. Timothy Struthers seemed to be unimpressed by his surroundings and undisturbed by his own carelessly worn suit and the necktie that had managed to creep around under his ear. When the big menus had been removed, he turned to the lawyer and said in a businesslike way, not subduing his resonant voice to the hushed atmosphere of the room, "I'm glad to have this opportunity to talk with you before meeting Natalie Netherfield—uh, I mean Mrs. Clifford. It would be a great help to get a general view of my subject from someone who has known her all her life, as I understand you have."

Fowler took his time in replying, studying the young man in a puzzled way. "Natalie greatly surprised me by writing that she had consented to permit a total stranger to do her biography, and especially to live in her house while gathering the material. She is the most private person I have ever known and long isolated from society by her illness. I can't for the life of me understand what material there is to be got from the life of a recluse, a life that, in a sense, has not been lived."

Young Struthers made no reply and his silence goaded Fowler into further speech. I had the curious feeling that the younger man was using tactics the lawyer himself generally employed.

"Of course," Fowler went on, "I suppose it was necessary to offer you hospitality while you collect your material. Alcott really has no facilities for overnight guests."

Overnight. He was hell-bent on getting rid of the young man who continued to devote himself to his lunch, occasionally giving the lawyer a deceptively bland look.

"Then too," Fowler said, "it certainly isn't customary to write the biography of a person who has only reached middle age—she is just forty—and from whom great things are yet to be expected. In Browning's words: 'The best is yet to be.' "

"We must all hope that is true," Struthers said politely. "There are two points you have made: one, that such a book would be an invasion of Mrs. Clifford's privacy. But in her poetry she has cried aloud her ecstasy over the progress of the love affair that transformed her life. Perhaps no love affair since that of Abelard and Héloise—which, I understand, is now regarded as apocryphal, at least the contributions of Héloise—and the Brownings, has been so well documented.

"The other point involves setting down the record while she is still comparatively young. The biography done in later life has the drawback that the sharp edges have worn off, much of the color has been dimmed, much that shaped the life and thought has been forgotten or, perhaps unintentionally, distorted to fit one's later image of oneself, to give past actions a more palatable quality."

There was nothing in Struther's comments at which Fowler could reasonably take umbrage, but I could feel his hostility. "What sort of material can you draw from the life of a woman who, up to two years ago, was an invalid, confined to her room, shut off from the world?"

Struthers thrust that unruly fair lock of hair off his forehead with an impatient gesture. "Well, of course, life isn't all action. The activities of the mind are exciting, too, as are the impulses behind human action. I was hoping, for instance, you could tell me what caused that long invalidism. There have been so many rumors, so much hearsay; her spine was cracked and she was permanently paralyzed; she had become a mystic and her verses were dictated to her by strange voices; she had withdrawn from the world because of a disappointment in love; she had become the devotee of some Oriental cult."

"If balderdash of that sort were to appear in a book about Natalie—" Fowler checked himself. "In any case, she simply would not permit such a publication to go on the market. There would be a lawsuit that would make a bankrupt of you and your publisher. That is the kind of distasteful scandalmongering you see in magazines sold in supermarkets for spiritual peeping Toms. They have no bearing on the life of a singularly lovely woman who, through no fault of her own, became an invalid for many years."

"What did happen to her, sir?" Struthers seemed completely impervious to atmosphere. His calm, unemotional tone was in sharp contrast with the anger that had overset the lawyer.

The latter restrained himself with a manifest effort. "Natalie was a beautiful, vibrant creature and at that time she was quite athletic. One afternoon she went swimming in the Sound, went out beyond her depth, and her mother, who was a strong swimmer, caught her and heaved her onto a raft, saving her life but injuring her spine. Unfortunately the exertion killed Mrs. Netherfield.

"Well, Natalie's belief that she was responsible for her mother's death was a shattering emotional shock. She simply withdrew into herself, withdrew from the world. Her sister's disappearance and the death not long after of her father left her with no one able to help her return to normal life. She lived all those years lying on a chaise longue in her little upstairs sitting room, seeing almost no one but her faithful maid, Alice Duke. And I sometimes think she'd have been better off without Alice, who has a jealous, over-protective attitude and encouraged Natalie to keep people away.

"Her only outlet was her poetry, and as she began to build a reputation and to become more widely known it might be said that in her case the truism held: Nothing succeeds like success. If she did not go out, the world came to her in the form of letters from admirers and fellow poets, flowers, gifts, tributes of all kinds. And, of course," and Fowler gave young Struthers a sour look, "the obscene kind of nonsensical rumors you've been mentioning began to circulate among a group of ignoramuses. And that is the story behind the legend of Natalie Netherfield, one of to-day's finest poets."

Fowler tackled roast beef in a concentrated way as though to indicate that the subject was closed. He had said all he had to say.

Struthers, who appeared to be an insensitive man, impervious to snubs, turned to me, though I was aware that he had kept me well within the line of his vision all the time. "Do you remember your aunt as she was during that long self-imposed exile?"

I stared at him. "Her illness began a year before I was born. I've never seen my aunt in my life. When my mother and father eloped, my mother was cast off by her father like something in a Victorian melodrama."

Struthers's tawny eyes narrowed as he studied me speculatively and I was aware that again my hostility had betrayed itself. "You know this whole setup strikes me as having a strong Victorian echo to it: the adamant father, the self-sacrificing mother, the daughter who elopes with a glamorous actor, the other daughter who becomes an imaginary invalid."

"It wasn't imaginary," Fowler said quickly, defensively.

"But surely it was excessive, what people now call over-reacting. I can understand a young girl's grief over her mother's death, particularly when the mother died saving her life, but I can't see her going into a twenty-year decline over it."

And, on second thought, neither could I. "It does seem excessive, doesn't it?"

Fowler made no comment. His attitude was one of a man who had divorced himself completely from the proceedings.

"I wonder," Struthers began, hesitated, and then went on more confidently. "You know, Miss Armstrong, I've seen some of those early movies your father made. Handsomest guy I've ever seen, on stage or off. Could it be that Natalie's problems arose out of thwarted love? Do you suppose she thought your father picked the wrong girl and resented it?"

I stared blankly at him. This was a new one to me.

Fowler came out of his self-imposed abstraction. "That is an infamous suggestion! One thing I must insist on. Neither of you, in any circumstances, is to hark back to the past. Natalie has suffered enough. It is high time she stays out in the sunlight and forgets that darkened room. She is happy now. For God's sake let her keep that way! She has done penance for twenty years for her supposed contribution to her mother's death. She is now prepared to share not only her home but her entire estate with an unknown niece to compensate for what she regards as an injustice, an injustice of which she was totally innocent. If you must write about her, write of the work that has made her so justly famous."

The lawyer had not raised his voice but there was a suppressed violence in it that shook me. His devotion to the interests of Natalie Netherfield Clifford went beyond that of lawyer and client, even beyond that of a lifelong friendship. That was what made Struthers's attitude the more outrageous. He had been making a workmanlike assault on his plate and appeared to be unaware of the cold dislike, almost the menace, in Fowler's voice. "You know, she strikes me as being one of those people who keep trying to strike a bargain with God. I'll do this for you if you'll do that for me. You see it all the time: women who built a reputation for generosity or great goodness when they are really trying to work off a debt to God."

The lawyer controlled himself with an effort. "Young man, when you have seen Natalie Netherfield for yourself, I'll expect you to withdraw those offensive words."

Old thick-skinned Struthers was not easily impressed or repressed. "I've taken a crash course in her poetry and read most of the critics. But there's one puzzle that stands out a mile. Who is this man who breached the fortified walls, threw open the windows, and not only set an invalid on her feet but swept her off on a round-the-world honeymoon? What's his background? Does he write too?"

We all refused dessert. Fowler signed the check and escorted us down to the street. His car would meet us at the Vanderbilt entrance to Grand Central Station in twenty minutes.

Struthers and I went down the stairs to the rotunda. He left me, grinning. "See you in twenty minutes and that doesn't mean twenty-one. Stay not on the order of your going but git." He winked at me and went off with long strides. When I returned, he was waiting at the top of the stairs. He saw me inching my way across the rotunda, struggling with three big suitcases and a dressing case, pushing them ahead of me, half kicking and half nudging them. He raced down the stairs to gather up the two heaviest cases.

"You should have told me."

Fowler's chauffeur had managed, in spite of a no-holds-barred contest from taxi drivers, to park a big Lincoln squarely at the entrance. He came around to collect the luggage and store it in the trunk while Fowler, after an automatic glance at his watch—we were on time to the second—waved us into the luxurious car.

As this was my first visit to New York I was too busily engaged in gathering new impressions, looking at glass and steel buildings sparkling in the sun, at the throngs of people who moved at a faster pace than they did in southern California, absorbing the excitement that was New York, to be in a mood to talk.

Struthers was made of different metal. He was there to get a story, and the story came first. "About Miss Nether-field—Mrs. Clifford's—husband," he said as though there had been no break in the conversation, "he must be a man of considerable means to take a world cruise for a honeymoon."

"He seems to be comfortably well off."

"I suppose by now," and Struthers grinned, "he is growing accustomed to being called Mr. Netherfield."

"I doubt it," Fowler said. "Clifford is very much a person in his own right. Perhaps not the demigod Natalie sees him as being, but impressive. He can hold his own without any difficulty."

"That must have been a determined assault he made on

the citadel. How did he manage to persuade her to receive him?"

"It started with letters, I believe, and in the end he wouldn't take no. Natalie has a—weakness, I suppose—for strong men. That was the great bond between her and her father. She admired his authoritarian manner. She is the kind of woman who wants to be subjugated by a male. A sort of horror of women's liberation. I heard her say once she was the kind of woman who is happy in bondage. But after her long seclusion she was afraid to meet Clifford for fear he had been attracted to a mirage and would be disappointed in the real woman. Fortunately it didn't work out that way. One meeting—and combustion!"

"He is considerably younger than she is, I understand."

I didn't know, of course, how people went about gathering material for books, but it struck me that this man Struthers was hunting for weak points and not for the stones on which to build.

"Yes, Clifford is somewhat younger. But the thing is that Natalie by her isolation from the world has retained her youth, almost her girlhood, while Clifford is more experienced, more mature in many ways, attractive, gay, virile, optimistic, perhaps the only man who could have roused Natalie and, in a sense, brought her back to life."

Fowler forestalled any more of Struthers's insistent questions. "By the way, you both come from California, don't you?"

"Hollywood," I said. "I had a job in a studio. Not acting. It was," and the old corrosive bitterness came through, "the studio where my father used to work. They took me in as an act of kindness."

Struthers looked at me and grinned. "Offhand I could think of at least a dozen more likely reasons."

"And you, Mr. Struthers?"

21

"San Francisco. At least that's home base. I do a bit of traveling, of course, to gather material, and I may have to put in a stretch in Hollywood after I finish this job."

"You make it sound like a jail sentence," I commented.

"Well, you know northern and southern California. Never the twain shall meet—if they can help it."

"Have you known each other long?" Fowler asked.

I shook my head, but Struthers said, "My loss, but it's not too late."

I did a double take. Fowler himself had introduced us. What kind of racket did he think we were in? Did he imagine some collusion between us?

"Mr. Struthers, may I ask who suggested you abandon your usual field and write the biography of a person who is not only a poet but a recluse?"

"My usual field?" Struthers spoke cautiously.

"When Natalie wrote that she had been persuaded to let you write her biography and said she had suggested that you, a complete stranger, stay in her house for an indefinite period to gather material, I naturally looked you up. You started as a crime reporter and turned to books. So far you have done three, which have had good sales and good reviews. You've stuck to the same theme: an account of unsolved murders, marshaling the available evidence and providing your own solution. Your most recent one, *The Filthy Witness*, has, I understand, been picked up for a series of television episodes. *Filthy Witness*. An unsavory title."

"It's from *Macbeth*. Remarkable, isn't it, how often blood is the theme of *Macbeth* and how rarely it is mentioned by name. Remember Lady Macbeth's 'Wash this filthy witness from your hand.' Blood that betrays the murderer's guilt."

Fowler, like Struthers, had a one-track mind. "From murder to poetry. Quite a jump, isn't it? As I asked before," he said with all the maddening persistence of a mosquito, "whose suggestion was this?"

I broke in excitedly as we turned west, and only later did it occur to me that Fowler thought I was running interference for Struthers, who needed my help about as much as he needed a wooden leg. "Oh, that's Carnegie Hall! I saw the sign. Do you suppose I could get down to New York now and then to hear music?"

"Naturally. You're a free agent, you know, Miss Armstrong." Fowler was irritated at my interruption. Then he said, "Oh, I suppose you inherited your mother's love of music."

"Her love, perhaps, but not her talent. She did her best to teach me but we had to sell the piano along with everything else when I was fifteen."

"You harbor a grievance too long. It's high time you forget it. Well, Mr. Struthers?"

"Oh, yes, you wanted to know what got me interested in Mrs. Clifford."

"And don't tell me it was her poetry, as you've just confessed to doing a cram course in it." This was less like a conversation than a cross-examination.

"Actually," Struthers said, "it was a former classmate of mine at Brown. We've kept in touch spasmodically by letter and now and then we meet either in San Francisco or in the District, where he now works, when I go to the Library of Congress for research. He thought I was getting in a rut and ought to devote myself for a change to a psychological mystery instead of murder cases filled with puzzles and unanswered questions." Struthers repeated thoughtfully, "Unanswered questions."

Three

Alcott was like a highly colored postcard illustration of a New England village at its most enchanting. New England, that is, before improvements had cut down the great elms and bulldozed the pre-revolutionary houses to make way for progress in the form of supermarkets and parking lots, soon to be outgrown and outmoded, but leaving ugly civilized scars as a reminder of what had been destroyed, a policy the town fathers called vision and looking ahead.

There was a village green running the length of Main Street, with a Congregational church whose slim spire thrust up through the gold and crimson and scarlet of autumn foliage at its most breathtaking. To a person from Southern California, with its bare brown hills, its desert only partially fertilized by a thin layer of soil washed down the Colorado River, its murky sky, this heart-stopping blaze of color, the vivid canopy of blue, the greenness, a distant view of rolling hills tree-clad, was shattering in its impact.

The green was lined with white colonial houses and a discreet plaque indicated that the village had been settled in 1706. That was the first moment in which I felt genuine gratitude for my aunt's munificence, for her gift of this beauty.

"Half of everything should belong to you," Aunt Natalie had written me six weeks earlier, "and I want you to have your mother's own room in her own home; your home now, I hope. I have so much to make up to you."

The house was a huge, square, three-story and attic, built in the late eighteenth century, set well back on ample grounds, a beautifully cared-for lawn, with maple, elm, and oak trees scattered over it, a mammoth hemlock whose branches swept the ground and, strategically and dramatically placed, a huge bush of so blazing a raspberry red that I gasped in sheer rapture. It was too much. I remembered Edna St. Vincent Millay's cry:

> . . . let fall
> No burning leaf; prithee, let no bird call.

A curving driveway led back, a long way back, to a three-car garage, converted from an old stable, one section of which held an ancient sleigh.

As the chauffeur drew the big car carefully up to the curb, a man came hurrying out of the house, dressed like any well-trained servant in a neat black jacket and well-pressed trousers, wearing a neat bow tie and well-polished shoes. He was so overweight that he almost wobbled and he had a huge, closely shaven face with features too small for it and bright eyes that were not those of a well-trained servant; they were sharp and probing, inquisitive and faintly impertinent.

He opened the car door while the chauffeur went around to collect the luggage from the trunk.

"Are you Bates?" Fowler asked.

"Yes, sir."

"Who hired you? Mrs. Clifford informed me only that a couple had been engaged and the old caretaker pensioned off."

"Agency," Bates said. "Old guy was getting past it, I guess. Miss Armstrong. Mr. Fowler. Mr. Struthers. All

25

present and accounted for." The well-trained act tended to slip a bit. "Everything is ready."

He led the way, wheezing as he tried to hasten his pace. In the open doorway stood an an angular woman who was probably in her middle thirties but looked older. She had a big shining nose and bad teeth and a somewhat horse-faced appearance, not improved by an unexpectedly elaborate hairdo. She too wore her neat black dress more like a costume than a uniform. An odd couple altogether, one that seemed faintly spurious.

The entrance was a delight, two stories high, with a staircase that curved along a side wall and across the hallway at the second-floor level. On the tesselated floor there were scatter rugs that might have been in a museum, and on a beautifully carved table set under an Italian mirror there was a high vase filled with chrysanthemums.

On the right a wide archway opened into a drawing room with white trim and exquisite wallpaper, which, I learned later, had been copied from that in a French château. There were magnificent rugs, priceless chairs, a heavily carved ornate table, and a magnificent lectern holding an illuminated manuscript. The room was so large that the concert grand piano framed by a picture window at one end was inconspicuous.

The air was scented with the spicy odor of potpourri from open Chinese jars. The room was stunning in its beauty but it lacked the "do not touch" quality one might have expected. These chairs and couches were meant to be sat on, the marble fireplace was for use and not mere ornament.

On the other side of the entrance double doors revealed a library with shelves to the ceiling, leather-bound books in open shelves, not sequestered behind glass, and deep chairs, two of which were drawn up near the fireplace in which birch logs had been stacked ready for lighting. This room too was designed for use as well as beauty. The lamps had been arranged not for effect but to throw the best light on tables and chairs.

"I am Freda Bates," the housekeeper said. "Shall I show you to your rooms or would you like tea first?"

Apparently no one wanted tea, so we trooped up the stairs with Mr. Fowler's taciturn chauffeur bringing up the rear, laden with luggage. Obviously Bates did not climb those stairs when he could avoid it, and I rather thought he was an expert at avoiding the unpleasant.

Freda indicated the doors at the right. "The Cliffords' suite, three rooms, all ready and waiting, even fresh flowers." The rooms at the back were assigned to Struthers and the lawyer. I was at the far left.

"Mrs. Clifford said you were to have the room with the piano, which was your mother's. The room is sound-proofed because she used to practice here. Shall I unpack for you?"

I didn't like her inquisitive expression and I didn't want her to realize that none of my clothes, with the exception of an old sweater and skirt and a beaten-up raincoat, had ever been worn before.

"Thanks, I can manage."

"This door is to your bath and the other one is your closet. When you've unpacked, just leave your luggage outside your door and Bates will take it up to the storeroom. Dinner's at seven and cocktails at six-thirty. Mrs. Clifford said no one bothers changing for dinner except on formal occasions. Well, if there's nothing else—"

"Nothing, thank you. Do you manage the cooking and run this big place all alone, Mrs. Bates?"

A look that revealed almost human feelings crossed the horse face. She patted the elaborate hairdo with stubby fingers, the thick thumb curling backward. "We've got a maid for the beds and dusting and she helps with the housework. A woman comes in twice a week for laundry and vacuuming and washing windows. All that. And, of course, Alice Duke is here now, but then I don't suppose she'll lift a hand unless it's for Mrs. Clifford, except to try to boss things. These personal maids! Been with her for twenty years and I can't imagine how she was persuaded to come home ahead of her lady. Probably thinks she'll fall apart without her help."

She sniffed, turned toward the door, muttered, "Oh, Lord, I forgot. Alice wanted to see Mr. Fowler the minute he came. It slipped my mind."

She closed the door and I was free to look around the room that had been my mother's for the first twenty-two years of her life and from which she had been exiled until her death.

I touched with gentle fingers the closed spinet and thought of the long hours of painstaking practice, of the promising, perhaps brilliant, career that she had sacrificed when she chose to follow her husband's way of life, and that had ended, before I was fifteen, in cheap lodgings where no piano was available.

Feeling like an intruder, I walked slowly around the room, wondering if my mother would have been pleased to have me here. There was a four-poster bed with pretty dimity hangings and an old-fashioned colorful patchwork quilt folded neatly at the foot. There was a rocking chair and a dainty dressing table and scatter rugs on wide waxed floorboards, and two casement windows with cushioned windowseats. One opened on the back garden where I saw the rose arbor and the hammock swung between the elm trees, which my mother had described. The other window opened on the side of the house, over the driveway. By leaning far out I could see the big garage and Mr. Fowler's chauffeur easing the Lincoln into the farthest stall. Because

28

of the warmth of the Indian summer both windows were wide open.

There was a large rack filled with music scores, on top of which there were family photographs: one of my grandfather, with the deep-socketed dark eyes of the Netherfields; one of my grandmother looking so much like my mother that if it had not been for the clothes and the way her hair was worn, I would have taken it for her. But it was autographed, "For my darling little Florence from her loving mother." She had the same light hair like a pale nimbus, the same small nose and indeterminate chin, the same placating smile, the same aura of defenselessness.

There were a dozen pictures of my father. The first, a studio photograph, was signed, "For Florence Netherfield with warm regards, George Armstrong." How handsome he had been! No woman could have resisted such fantastic good looks and so much charm. The last picture, a candid camera shot, was signed, "For my little sweetheart from her adoring George."

To my surprise there was a photograph of me and for a moment I wondered how on earth Aunt Natalie could have got hold of it. Perhaps, after all, my mother, knowing how serious her condition was, had tried to heal the breach with her sister. Then I realized with a shock that the girl in the photograph was not I. The dress was in the fashion of twenty years ago, as was the style of the hair. This must be Aunt Natalie. I looked from the photograph to the mirror. No wonder Mr. Fowler had been surprised, that he had said I carried my identification with me.

I lifted the cover from the bed, slipped off my shoes, and lay down, tired from the long trip from California, the tension of meeting the unknown, the realization that I had burned my bridges behind me and saw no clear future ahead, and the bitter thoughts that too long had corroded a nature that was meant, I thought, to be cheerful.

There had been some surprises. Mr. Fowler had proved to be not only hostile but suspicious of me and of my motives. At least he had been unable to doubt my identity. But he had disliked and distrusted Mr. Struthers too. He had tried to discover what had prompted the young man to write my aunt's biography. An unlikely subject, one would suppose, for a man whose specialty was unsolved murders.

II

I must have drifted into a light doze, but I was aroused by a tap at the door. I was about to call "Come in," when I heard the door next to mine open. My room might be soundproofed but apparently all the windows were open to catch the last warmth of the season.

I heard Fowler say, "Well, Alice, you're looking well. I hope you left Mrs. Clifford in good shape. I understand you want to see me. Oh," testily, "sit down; sit down."

"Well, I don't hardly know where to start," the woman said. "And maybe it's nothing at all. But I thought, if I should be right, I'd better see you about it. You'd know what to do. So when Miss—Mrs. Clifford suggested I come home ahead of them to get their suite in shape and make sure the right things were in this writer's room and the girl who claims to be her niece—"

"She is her niece," Fowler said dryly.

"Well, I figured that at least I'd ease my mind."

"Mrs. Clifford isn't well?" Fowler asked in quick alarm.

"Oh, no, she's like a new woman. Alive and self-confident and glowing. Like a bride. Well, of course, for all her being forty, she is a bride and still almost like a girl. And that happy!"

"Fine. Then what's got you in such a dither, woman?"

"It's—well—I hope you won't think I'm imagining

things, but you know how it is. Mr. Clifford is a mighty good-looking man and he's a lot younger than her and women make a fuss over him. Not," she added hastily, "that he doesn't seem devoted. More devoted all the time. And proud of her. When people want to meet her and ask for her autograph, he just beams. I have to say this," and she spoke reluctantly, "if he's done any straying, he's been almighty careful about it. As he should be, with her being older and not used to happiness, as you might say, and she's got a jealous streak. Not that exactly but just—well, not sure if she can go on holding him, if you know what I mean."

Fowler was being patient with an effort. "What is actually worrying you?"

"Well, first there was that bad fish that gave her ptomaine in Marseilles. If it hadn't been for quick work by a doctor in the hotel, she wouldn't have been saved. And then there was the fall. They were climbing in the Alps—"

"Natalie climbing!"

"Well, just sort of scrambling along, but I know what you mean. You wouldn't hardly think it was possible for love to perform such a miracle. Why, once she climbed more than a hundred steps up a church tower, keeping right behind him."

"Good God!"

"I know, and none the worse for wear except she was tired and had bad cramps in her legs the next day. I ask you! No exercise for years and then off she goes on a jaunt like that before her muscles have a chance to get trained for it. Well, anyhow, to get back to the point."

"Let's do that."

"They were looking out at the view when she slipped and fell right off the side of the mountain. Oh, no, she wasn't badly hurt. That was the miracle. There was a hidden ledge not a foot down and she landed on that. Just bruised and scared. Mr. Clifford was wild. Carried her down himself and wouldn't be satisfied until the doctor swore up and down there was no serious injury, nothing broken, no internal damage."

"Well?"

There was a prolonged pause that Fowler did nothing to break. It dawned on me that I was eavesdropping, but it never occurred to me to close my window. Instead, I held my breath, listening.

"Well, you know Mrs. Clifford. Always a bit superstitious, what with her lucky piece and her crystal gazers and the ones who claim to know the stars and the occult. She didn't say anything when I spoke to her about the accidents, except once she said in an odd tone, 'Things come in threes. I wonder about the next time.'"

Fowler's control slipped. "And why in hell's name did you tell Mrs. Clifford you thought she—you thought he—"

"It was my duty," Alice said virtuously.

"You should have known better. After all, you admit Clifford is devoted to his wife. What right had you to jump to such an unspeakable conclusion?"

"I didn't really. I just sort of wondered. That's all. And I didn't lay the blame to anyone. I didn't say they weren't just accidents. But it was my duty to put her on her guard like."

"Against what?"

Alice was not to be pushed and she was obviously offended at not having her story taken in the horrified spirit she had anticipated. "Mrs. Clifford didn't discuss it at all for several days, but she was sort of withdrawn, more like the way she used to be. Then one day she asked me to accompany her to some man she'd heard about who could see into the future, some sort of occultist."

Fowler groaned.

"Anyhow this man we went to see wasn't a bit what

you'd expect. No gypsy stuff, no 'cross my palm with silver' or making passes over her head and telling her to relax in the infinite, like some we've gone to. She always takes me with her because you never know but what some of them might be fakes. Up to something, you know. This man was dressed like anyone in a plain business suit. He read the cards and told her that she had achieved great fame. Then he swept the cards away and looked at the crystal ball. A long time. Then he stood up and said, 'I am sorry. There is nothing more I can tell you.' "

Alice went on with her story, quoting verbatim.

" 'They told me you can see into the future.'

" 'Sometimes the curtain lifts a little. That is all.'

"Mrs. Clifford didn't move. Then she said, 'I want to know.'

" 'There is a picture forming. Slowly. Murky. There is danger in it.'

"And she asked, 'What kind of danger? Anything I can avoid?'

"And after a while he said, 'It can still be avoided.'

" 'What can?'

" 'The knife. But I must warn you to be very careful. Very wise, madam.'

"So she paid him, and it was nearly seventy-five dollars in American money, and we went away."

"I suppose," Fowler said, "Mrs. Clifford's picture had appeared in the papers as a visiting celebrity, and some mention made of that near accident in the Alps."

"Well, yes."

"So the chances are this charlatan knew who she was."

"I suppose so." Alice was definitely sulky now. Her big play had misfired. "Anyhow there haven't been any accidents since then. But I found out Mrs. Clifford was planning to change her will and have this unknown niece come here, though why she should care what happened to Florence's child, I don't know, not after the way Florence acted; and then she agreed to let some man come and stay here to write up her life. And on top of all that they hired this couple, the Bateses. For my money they've never been servants before in their lives. A nest of vipers. That's what Mrs. Clifford is coming home to, if you ask me."

"Well, I didn't. However, thank you for telling me about it. But in the future, bring your suspicions to me before unloading them on Mrs. Clifford."

"Just the same—"

"All right. All right. We'll do our best to keep her safe. And at least," Fowler added dryly, "she has been warned."

Alice's voice broke. "You think I'm a silly old woman and my nose is out of joint because of this Mr. Clifford and the way she worships him, but I love her as though she was my own child." The door closed behind her.

"God!" Fowler muttered. "God! God! God!" And then he noticed the open casement and hastened belatedly to close the window.

Four

Even the cocktails prepared by Bates failed to warm the atmosphere in the big drawing room before dinner. Even the excellent meal—I had misjudged Mrs. Bates; whatever her failings might be, she was an inspired cook—could not create a congenial mood. In part this was due to the fact that the three of us were seated at a long table that practically required a walkie-talkie for communication. The dining room was L-shaped, with a smaller section which held a table for four. I thought we've have been better off there.

Not that there was any lack of conversation, but it was all at cross-purposes. Mr. Fowler single-mindedly hammered at Struthers, determined to know what had instigated his interest in Natalie Netherfield. Struthers was equally insistent on learning what made Clifford tick, what kind of man had been able to sweep off her feet a woman who was practically a recluse.

The suspicion and hostility between the two men was unconcealed and disagreeable.

Once Struthers shifted his line of questioning. "How well did you know the Netherfield family, Mr. Fowler?"

"My father was Mr. Netherfield's lawyer and I took over when my father died."

"Was Netherfield as much the heavy father, the Browning type, as he sounds?"

Fowler deliberated. "He was not a reasonable man, almost a violent man at times. I always had the impression that there was a streak of violence held under control, but just barely. I felt sorry for his wife, who wasn't the kind to assert herself."

"Easily browbeaten?"

"In a way. Loud voices and angry arguments frightened her. Bluster subdued her."

"Did it subdue his daughters too?" The question was spoken so smoothly that Fowler fell into the trap.

"Of course, there was never any question of bluster where Natalie was concerned. She was his favorite. He was proud of her beauty and then, when she became an invalid, he wrapped her in cotton wool. Too much so, perhaps."

"You mean he encouraged that invalidism in order to keep her at home?"

Fowler weighed his words. "I doubt if he ever thought of it in those terms, but there's an element of truth. He was a possessive man."

"And the other daughter—Florence?"

"She was more like her mother's side of the family. Of course, she had an outlet in her music. She was good. Very good."

"But he wasn't as proud of her talent as he was of Natalie's?"

"It wasn't like that. To begin with, Natalie did not start writing until after her father's death. Netherfield was extremely proud when Florence made her Town Hall debut. It was a kind of reflected glory for him. What caused his hostility was the shock when she married George Armstrong."

"Why should he be shocked?" Struthers asked. "There was nothing wrong with Armstrong—then. He was at his peak, a superb actor with a tremendous following."

"Netherfield was—unreasonable. Violently unreasonable. That's really all I have to say about it, Struthers, and it has no place in Natalie's story."

"I wonder." But Struthers let the subject drop.

As soon as coffee had been served, I excused myself on the pretext of fatigue and said I'd pick up some books in the library and go to bed for an early night.

"Very wise of you," Fowler said. "Tomorrow will probably be hectic with Natalie's arrival and all the reporters and inquisitive neighbors, and Lord knows what."

"Good heavens, I had not thought of that."

Again I saw the odd expression in the lawyer's eyes. "You don't seem to have grasped your aunt's position, Miss Armstrong, or to have the slightest conception of her fame. She is undoubtedly America's leading poet and, because of the Pulitzer Prize and the nonsense printed about her illness and her romantic marriage, she will be besieged by reporters, critics, interviewers, photographers, not to speak of curious neighbors and people eager to follow in the train of a celebrity. She was abroad at the time the award was given and, so far, the American media hasn't had a chance to talk to her. And, of course, with her unusual beauty, everyone will want a picture of her."

Having given me all the attention necessary, Mr. Fowler ostentatiously withdrew to the library, where he took out a small traveling chessboard and the day's chess problem torn from a newspaper, indicating that he had no further interest in talking with either of us.

Balked at a chance of picking out some books because Mr. Fowler had made clear it would be an intrusion for anyone to enter the library, I stood hovering uncertainly at the foot of the staircase. Struthers said, "Look here, it's a wonderful night and there won't be many more like this. Let's take a little walk along the green and get some fresh air and exercise."

"Well—"

He grinned disarmingly. "I am tame, pronounce."

I capitulated to his grin. It was pleasant to have one friendly person in the house. "I'll get my coat."

It was not, after all, as warm as I had expected after the balmy day. There was a real bite in the air and the leaves were beginning to stir as though whispering to each other.

"One big storm and they'll be gone," Struthers commented as he shortened his stride and strolled beside me along the green, past the lovely old houses, many of which had left their windows unshaded so that we could see lights inside and people reading or talking or watching television.

"I like this, don't you?" Struthers said. "A world that has no dread of people looking in the windows. Nice and predictable." As I chose that moment to stumble over a dead branch and lose my balance, he laughed as he caught my arm to steady me.

"Nice and predictable," I said. "There's no place like that this side of heaven, Mr. Struthers."

"The name's Timothy," he said. "Tim takes less breath, though I will answer to hi or any loud cry."

"Do you always talk in quotations?"

"Usually. It saves thinking for myself, Miss Armstrong."

The studied formality in his tone made me laugh. "All right, you win. My name is Constance."

"Usually called Connie?"

"No, I've never had a nickname."

"Nonsense. Everyone has a nickname. We'll have to invent one. What about Kate?"

"Why Kate?"

"Why not?"

I found myself laughing again.

"That's better," he said approvingly. "You ought to laugh more. Looked to me there for a while as though you had lost the habit."

As I tried to draw my arm away, his hand tightened. "Don't be like that, Kate," he said cajolingly. "You know

38

what? We'd better strike up a friendly alliance if we're going to find ourselves in a nest of vipers."

That was what Alice had said. "So your window was open too."

"Mine too," he agreed, and I could hear the smile in his voice. He added unexpectedly, "I wish it weren't so dark. I can't make out your expression and I can't see your eyes."

"What difference does that make?"

He answered obliquely, "You know, Kate, before we are done I'm going to get to the bottom of that bitterness of yours and root it out. It's corrosive, my dear. It can play tricks on you, warp you. Hatred is one of the poisons; like jaundice, it alters the true colors of things."

This time I managed to free my arm. "Did you bring me out to preach to me?"

"I brought you out because you have the most wonderful eyes in the world. They shook me. Any man—well, this isn't the time for that, is it? I have insatiable curiosity and I want to know what is turning a delightful girl, at least one who is potentially delightful, into an embittered woman. Watch it, Kate."

I turned on my heel and started back to the house and he accompanied me, silent this time. There was no sound but the occasional brittle rustle as we stepped on fallen autumn leaves. As the wind began to rise, I pulled my coat closer around me. Then I felt a few drops of rain on my head. The last half block we quickened our pace. I was about to lift the polished knocker when Tim reached around me and opened the door.

"I unlocked it before we left. I didn't expect we'd return so early."

Mr. Fowler glanced up from his chessboard as we came in, looking from face to face, searching for God knows what. Probably for evidence that we had, between us, been concocting some plan for the general undoing of Natalie

Netherfield Clifford.

I marched into the library, undeterred by Mr. Fowler's eyes. If I didn't assert myself, I'd end by being afraid of him. My aunt's three books of poems and a volume marked REVIEWS were bound in blue leather with a design in silver. About this I did my aunt an injustice. The books had been bound in her honor by her publisher and not by her for her own aggrandizement. I gathered them up and said, "Good night, Mr. Fowler. Good night, Tim."

Fowler's brows rose but he said "Good night" in a colorless voice.

"I think," Tim said, "I'd better check on the windows in case the Bateses have forgotten them. We're in for a real storm, rain and high wind, if I know my stuff. Too bad Mrs. Clifford will miss the peak of the autumn foliage."

"Good idea," Fowler approved. "The Bateses have an apartment over the garage and the maid has a room at one end of the attic which has been finished, bath and all. At least, Natalie will be spared the storm. She is terrified of storms, loses all control. It's one weakness with which her father had no patience."

Tim had been right. Dead leaves rattled against the casement windows, which shook under the force of the gathering wind. I settled down in bed with the reading light comfortably adjusted and opened the earliest of Natalie Netherfield's books of verse. It was called *Pegasus,* a slim volume with one short poem to a page, none of them running more than three or four quatrains, some of them only a couple of lines. They were a girl's poems with an unmistakable voice coming through. This was Natalie herself speaking, tentatively as yet, but with her own voice. Here and there was a touch of the sleeping princess waiting to be awakened by a lover's kiss, but no Brunhilda awaiting the lover to plunge through fire to arouse her. Fire was out of Natalie's orbit; she was more at home with starlight.

There were some memorable lines, sharply perceptive, but the love poems were, I felt sure, addressed to quite imaginary lovers. Nonetheless the book had vitality and charm and it was eminently quotable. When I turned to the book of clippings, I saw that the majority of critics likened her work to the early Millay, but a Millay from the chaste purlieus of Gramercy Park rather than the Greenwich Village of the twenties.

The wind had risen and there was an occasional sharp crack as a dead branch fell onto the roof. Once the light flickered and then was bright again. The rain was drumming on the windows now and the room was chillier. I pulled a soft blanket up over my bare shoulders.

The second book, *Scorched Earth*, had been written ten years later, written after she had become an invalid and a recluse. Written when legends had begun to arise about her and occasional poems appeared in magazines, attracting a small but growing and fervent cult. The poet of the first book had looked through the casement at life. In the second book one glimpsed a smoldering fire, an authentic passion, a tumult of emotion incompatible with the physical isolation in which the girl had lived. Girl? Woman now. The reviewers of this book compared her with Emily Dickinson. There was an oddly disturbing quality about them. This was not the Lady of Shalott's "I am half sick of shadows." This was a tormented woman in revolt.

I had left one of the windows open a crack and I got up to close it; too late, I realized, as my bare foot stepped on a soaked rag rug, which I went to hang over the shower rod. For a moment I stood looking out at the wind-swept green, what I could see of it by the dim glow of street lights through a curtain of rain.

The last book, *Prismed Light,* had appeared nine months earlier, three months after her marriage. It was a sonnet sequence, written by an author for whom fashions in verse

41

had no meaning, a poet who had come into her own and had confidence in her own medium. She felt no need to follow trends. She poured out her emotion, disciplined now, finely honed and brilliant, as though she had etched each word in fire. This was the awakening of the recluse, the flinging open of the casement on life, the change from invalid to glowing woman, the miracle caused by love, so transcendent a love, so passionately expressed, that reading it was an unforgettable experience. Inevitably the reviewers compared her work with the *Sonnets from the Portuguese*, and not to the advantage of Elizabeth Barrett Browning. Critics feel more comfortable when they can fit things into neat categories, like packaged goods on a foodstore shelf. It spares the painful necessity of breaking new ground and applying a personal judgment.

The picture that emerged of Jack Clifford, the man who had wrought the miracle and brought Natalie Netherfield to life, was highly colored. Brave, true, noble, unselfish, charming beyond expression, a lover to sweep any woman off her feet, the source of all strength, all tenderness, all delight. And through it all ran the thread of incredulous wonder that this love should have come to her.

I remembered Browning's wry comment, years after the death of his wife: "That was a strange and heavy burden, that wreath of sonnets."

What must it be like for a man to go through life placarded as the recipient of a woman's adoration? To have to live up eternally to that kind of image must be intolerable. An older woman, too. Probably as the years passed, her age would be more apparent while he remained young and virile and, presumably, attractive to, attracted by, women. But would such a burden, could such a burden, lead a man to attempt to destroy the woman, as Alice had suggested?

I'll know when I see them in the morning, I thought. I put down *Prismed Light* and turned my head on the cool pillowslip after switching off the bedside lamp.

Outside the night seemed to draw closer with the fury of wind and rain beating at the casements as though determined to get in.

Once I roused when quiet feet went up the stairs and the door next to mine closed. Mr. Fowler must have solved his chess problem. Once I started bolt upright when there was a terrific crash.

After that there was nothing at all but an awareness, deep down, that I was safe and warm and comfortable and that tomorrow, at least, held nothing to worry about. I no longer heard my mother's rasping breath; I no longer wondered—with what agony—where my father was and if he was fed and under shelter; I did not dread the morning when some stubborn man in the studio would urge me to let him prove that I was photogenic, tell me I was wasted at a typewriter, that I should follow in my father's footsteps. This lovely feeling must be the thing they called security. No wonder my sleep that night was dreamless.

Five

Next morning, after a hasty shower, I dressed quickly in the new leaf-green sweater and skirt I had bought in Los Angeles on Aunt Natalie's money. The warmth of the sweater was comforting because the room was chilly and the water in the shower had been barely lukewarm. When I went downstairs I discovered that the tree which had crashed in the night had brought down power lines and the house had been without electricity until a few hours ago.

Bates had lighted fires in the big drawing room and the library to counteract the chill, and breakfast was served at the table in the small end of the L of the dining room. Here a bar had been installed along with a wine rack and a small machine for making ice and a gadget for crushing ice cubes.

This morning Mr. Fowler looked pinched and cold and as though he had not slept. Tim, in wool slacks and turtleneck sweater, tackled ham and eggs and orange juice enthusiastically. Bates, trundling cumbersomely around the table, looked aggrieved. Tim grinned at me when Bates filled his coffee cup for the third time.

"I have a big body to feed." He looked out of the window onto the lawn. "Hard to believe it's the same world, isn't it?"

The force of wind and rain had driven most of the leaves from the trees, leaving a few dejected clumps here and there, but most of the trees were stripped and bare, with a multicolored carpet covering the lawn that had been green the day before. The sky that had been so piercingly blue was a leaden gray and rain was still falling; not the downpour of the night but a steady, relentless, sodden rain.

"At least," Mr. Fowler said in a tone of satisfaction, "weather like this will discourage any curious neighbors or sightseers. Natalie would have hated all that fuss." He glanced at his watch. "Nine o'clock. They can hardly get here for another hour. It's always difficult to find taxis around the airports at that unlikely hour. They'll probably take a bus to Manhattan and a taxi from there."

But he was wrong. The swinging door to the butler's pantry was flung open unceremoniously, and a stout, gray-haired woman burst into the dining room.

"They're here," she said. "They're here!" She looked at me with much the same shock the lawyer had displayed the day before. For a moment there was a kind of disbelief and then something like hatred. She hurried to fling open the front door, letting in wind and rain and cold air.

"Don't keep the door open, Alice," Fowler called irritably. "You're chilling the whole house." As there was no reply, he grumbled, "The woman's a silly, hysterical fool," and I wondered how much of the uncharacteristic outburst was an attempt to convince himself. Evidently the maid's belief that Clifford had twice attempted to kill his wife had contributed to the lawyer's sleepless night.

He flung down his napkin and pushed back his chair. Automatically Tim and I followed his example and then hesitated. After all, we were strangers here, so we went into the library, from which we could see the taxi at the curb, see the tall man who helped a slight woman to alight and then, with an arm around her, shielding her as best he could from the rain, he ran with her to the door.

"Natalie running!" Fowler said in a tone of disbelief. "Natalie running!"

Then I heard her voice, warm, low-pitched, beautiful. "Brendon, my dear! How wonderful to see you. Oh, don't bother, Alice. I'm perfectly all right."

"You ought to get out of those wet things. You'll catch your death of cold," Alice grumbled.

Natalie laughed. "My poor Alice! I can never convince you that I am well now."

I found myself wondering whether Alice, like old Mr. Netherfield, would have been happier to keep Natalie an invalid, whether her instinctive distrust of me could be founded on the fact that I might replace her in Natalie's affections and confidence. Bitterness, as Tim had pointed out, might be a poison, but so was possessiveness, and of the two it was probably the more potentially dangerous.

"Here," Natalie protested, "what on earth are you trying to do?"

"Just step out of those wet shoes and into these warm slippers."

This time Natalie's laughter was echoed by a man's ringing, joyous laugh, so infectious that I found myself smiling in sympathy; but Tim, I noticed, was listening intently and there was no trace of amusement on his face.

"Mrs. Clifford," I heard Mrs. Bates say, "would you like some coffee or would you rather have some breakfast?"

"You must be Mrs. Bates. I am so glad you have come to help us out. Will you ask your husband to give the taxi driver a hand? I'm afraid there is rather a lot of luggage. Alice, I don't need to ask whether our suite is ready. You never fail."

"Let's not stand here, darling," Clifford said. "I see a roaring fire in the drawing room. Nice of you to come, Mr. Fowler."

"Brendon," Natalie said, "how about Constance? Is she here? And the writer—Mr. Struthers, I think."

"Both here," he said, "but perhaps I should warn you—"

On cue Tim and I crossed the big entrance hall and went into the drawing room. I found myself looking at Aunt Natalie. This wasn't the girl in the photograph. This was what twenty years of illness had made of her. The huge dark eyes were sunken, the passionate mouth had lost something of its fullness and the corners were tucked in, there was a deep groove down either cheek. She's old, I thought, out of the arrogance of my twenty years.

She came to press a fragrant cheek against mine. "Dear Constance, welcome home. I want you to be happy here. Very happy."

"I don't know how to thank you, Aunt Natalie."

"Just Natalie," she said quickly. "It's more—friendly." She touched her husband's arm. "And this is my Jack."

He might not be the demigod of *Prismed Light,* but he was a most attractive man with a flash of white teeth in a face bronzed by outdoor life, and a virile self-confidence that explained how he had managed to sweep this woman out of darkness and into the light. He smiled at me and then bent over to kiss my cheek lightly.

Natalie's great dark eyes peered closely at me and I realized that she was extremely nearsighted. Then for what seemed an endless moment she stared at me, her hand outstretched not in welcome but as though to thrust me away.

"Why, you are my youth," she said, her voice almost a whisper. "I didn't know—I didn't realize—I expected you to be like Florence."

"You're enough alike to be sisters," Clifford said, and the glow came back to her face.

She turned to Tim, lounging in the doorway, one hand in his pocket, one pushing back that lock of hair. "And you, I think, must be Timothy Struthers about whose work I've been hearing such exciting things."

He took the small hand she held out to him. "This is a pleasure to which I've been looking forward, Miss Netherfield."

"Mrs. Clifford," she reminded him. "I want you to know my husband. And this, Jack, is Mr. Struthers who," and she smiled mischievously, "is going to immortalize me."

"You have done that for yourself, darling," Clifford said.

The taxi driver dropped luggage inside the hallway, took a swift look around, pocketed the money Bates gave him and returned to his cab, running through the rain.

Clifford looked at the wheezing houseman, whose raincoat dripped on the floor. "Are you Bates?"

"That's right."

"I hope you and your wife are comfortably settled. Mrs. Clifford told me the apartment over the garage is completely furnished. Have you got the help you need? All that?"

"Everything's fine." Bates added belatedly, "Sir."

"Good. You might get this stuff up to our rooms and ask Alice to unpack my wife's suitcases. I can handle my own." The telephone in the library rang and he started toward it and then hesitated.

"Answer it, dear," Natalie called. "This is your house now."

I found myself wondering if he would resent being reminded that he now had a stake in the house.

While he was answering the telephone, Fowler said, "I can't take my eyes off you, Natalie. You're a different woman. When I think back a couple of years—"

"Don't," she said quickly; "it's like going from death to life. All those wasted years!"

"Not wasted. You had your poetry and your growing fame."

"But the best poetry came, as everything has come, from Jack."

48

"You are a happy woman."

"Sometimes it frightens me, being so happy." She turned to smile radiantly at Tim. "Happy lives, like happy countries, are without any history. I'm afraid you will find this job dull and disappointing."

"Then it could only be my fault," he assured her. "I can't wait to get started."

"Give me a day or two to settle down. My husband and I have been traveling for almost a year, stopping here and there for a few days, at most a few weeks. I've crammed a whole life into those months and I haven't had time to digest it yet."

"But it isn't a travelogue I'm after, it's you."

Her lovely smile made her seem years younger, almost wiped out the signs of age and illness and years. "Would you pluck out the heart of my mystery?"

"If I can," he said soberly.

"You must consider yourself free to do as you like, you know, until we can arrange some sort of schedule. Is your room comfortable?"

"It couldn't be better."

"I asked Alice to make sure you had a good desk and chair and working light, but don't hesitate to ask for anything you need. And at least you'll have some companionship." She smiled at me. "You've got acquainted already, haven't you?"

I made no comment and Tim said noncommittally, "Well, we've met."

Fowler gave him a sharp look, but Natalie did not notice our mutual nonenthusiasm. She turned her head as her husband appeared in the doorway. The moth to the candle. The needle to the north.

"That was Perkins, darling. He planned to meet your plane—"

"At six-thirty in the morning!"

"The weather discouraged him, but he'd like to come out this afternoon, if you'll let him."

"But there is nothing to discuss. I haven't a book ready. And it's more than a two-hour drive from New York. And the weather—"

"I suspect it's publicity. He wants to bring Fosdick from the *Times*, who'd like to do a feature story on you."

"But there's nothing really—"

"Better let them come, dear. Get it over with. After all," Clifford grinned at her, "a celebrity is at the mercy of her public."

She laughed. "Don't be absurd, Jack. Oh, all right, let them come. But not to lunch. I must rest for a couple of hours. I never sleep well on planes." The great dark eyes swept over us. "You'll forgive me? I'll probably have a tray in my room, but please feel at liberty to do exactly as you please. And, Brendon, if you have any dreary business to discuss, put it off until tomorrow, will you?"

"Of course, Natalie. There's nothing to worry you. A few questions about your holdings and the new will to sign, unless you have changed your mind about doing anything so drastic. I am a great believer in second thoughts in these matters."

She kissed his cheek. "It will be all right. I'm well and happy, Brendon." She went slowly up the stairs with a cheerful wave of the hand. Clifford concluded his telephone conversation, followed her up the stairs, and somewhere above a door closed.

II

The hours dragged on, the sullen rain turning the fallen leaves to a sodden mass, the wind now and then hurling rain against a windowpane with an angry sound. Bates was installing storm windows, and from what I could see, he

50

resented it bitterly. Fowler had taken possession of the library and was engrossed in one of his eternal chess problems. Tim, wearing a raincoat, his head bare, went for a walk. This time he did not ask me to accompany him.

In my room, the windows closed, secure in the effectiveness of the soundproofing, I opened the little piano, ran my fingers over the keys, and discovered that it had recently been tuned. Aunt Natalie had overlooked nothing to make me comfortable and happy. After that startled, dismayed moment when the cry, *Why, you are my youth,* had been wrenched from her, she had been all warmth and graciousness. The resemblance had shocked her, as the change in her from that youthful photograph had shocked me, but one question had been answered. She was profoundly in love with her husband and he gave every evidence not only of bearing up under the weight of that much-publicized adoration, but he seemed genuinely devoted and proud of her. Certainly the speed with which he had remarked that we were like sisters had been exactly the right thing to say in the circumstances. It had eased the moment of pain she had experienced at the sight of her lost youth, particularly in the presence of her young husband.

I crouched beside the rack of piano scores and looked them over. Most of them were far beyond my reach: the Bach *Chromatic Fantasy,* the Chopin études, the Schubert *Wanderer.* I could remember my mother playing that or trying to play it after her technique had begun to slip away. How very good she must have been when she made her Town Hall debut.

After her death I had found the reviews tucked away in a big envelope that also held my father's love letters: "Sound technique . . . a broad grasp of the composer's intentions . . . maturity and exceptional power for so young a woman. This is a career to watch, an experience to remember."

51

I settled for one of the simpler Schubert impromptus, playing slowly, my fingers stiff and cumbersome, gave up and tackled the third Chopin Prelude, playing each note of the left hand slowly, slowly, remembering my mother's reiterated admonition: *Festina lente.* I'd never be any good, always an amateur, but with an opportunity to practice and take lessons I could improve enough for my own private enjoyment and perhaps master some of the less difficult Beethoven sonatas.

The tap at the door surprised me. The morning had slipped past and Bates had come to announce lunch. It was a silent meal, on the whole, as neither of the Cliffords put in an appearance and their private thoughts absorbed Tim and Fowler, preventing any display of hostility between them.

When we got up from the table, Fowler said, "By the way, Struthers, I think you had better attend the interview session this afternoon. You may pick up some pointers."

"Thank you. I'd appreciate that."

As Fowler had more or less appropriated the library for his own use, I went up to my room, but I had tired myself at the piano and I had already read Aunt Natalie's books. I made a mental note to return them to the library, but I must be careful not to let her know I had never read them before, that my mother had rarely spoken of her younger sister. Apparently there had been hostility between them. I began to suspect, from Alice's hints, that my mother had, unexpectedly, been the aggressor. That she had more or less engineered the elopement for fear of competition from Natalie. It did not seem like her but, of course, children are never able really to see their parents.

The rain had become a mere drizzle as I bundled up in my worn raincoat and boots and went out. An advantage of naturally curly hair is that rain does not affect it. Only out of doors did I feel free to think. I saw now that there might be two sides to the Netherfield conflict. For the first time since I was fifteen I was freed of my bitterness toward the Netherfields.

Another thing I had learned. There could be no possible foundation for Alice's suspicion that Jack Clifford had attempted to kill his wife. The idea was unthinkable. He was genuinely devoted to her; gratitude in part, perhaps, for her adoration; but real pride in her fame, and I felt he responded genuinely to that irresistible charm of hers, an elusive quality that had partly to do with that sudden illuminating smile, partly with another-world vision behind the great brooding eyes. I decided that I liked Jack Clifford very much indeed.

I walked the length of the green, up one side and down the other, looking at the houses, stopping to watch men busy with tackle and a chain saw, cutting up the massive elm that had fallen on the power lines. I explored some little side streets and fell in love with a small, dark house that must have been built in the mid-nineteenth century.

When I got back, I saw two cars drawn up at the curb: a sleek Cadillac and a small foreign job with ALCOTT RE-PORTER in big letters on the side. Evidently the interview was in progress. I hesitated about going in but I thought I could slip up to my room unnoticed.

At first the drawing room seemed to be filled with people, but there were only seven men and Aunt Natalie, who was wearing a deep red velvet housecoat, her hair swept up the way I wore mine, and a faint perfume that had the spicy smell of carnations.

It was Jack Clifford who caught sight of me first in my bedraggled raincoat, my hair plastered to my head and cheeks. "Come in, Constance, and meet all these nice people: Mr. Perkins, who is Natalie's publisher; Mr. Fosdick of *The New York Times;* Mr. Kent, editor of the Alcott *Reporter;* and his photographer, Mr. Wilson. Come on in."

Fowler compressed his lips but made no comment. Tim, who was sitting on the piano bench at the far end of the room, gave me an encouraging nod, and Natalie said in her lovely voice, "Of course, dear."

I moved back to the end of the room near Tim to indicate that I too was a mere spectator.

It was *The New York Times* man who said, "Miss Netherfield, I hope you won't think this a foolish question, but do you have any particular method of work, any special approach to your poetry? I won't ask, 'Where do you get your inspiration?' "

She laughed at that. "Thanks for small blessings."

"Do you conceive the poem as a whole? Do you do much rewriting?"

"May I interrupt, please?" the young photographer said. "Before the light changes, I have to get some pictures of the tree that fell on the green and cut off power last night. May I take my pictures now?"

The *Times* man looked resigned. The editor from the local paper said hastily, "I'm sure Miss Netherfield will understand."

"Of course, though I'm rather afraid of photographers, you know."

"You needn't be," the young photographer said fervently. "You look just the way I've always imagined a poetess would look."

Natalie laughed at that but said firmly, "Poet, not poetess."

"I'd like one of you sitting just as you are, beside the fire, and maybe holding one of your books."

"No," she said firmly.

"But—"

Jack Clifford smiled. "The lady says no; she means no."

"If you'd just turn this way, not quite so far, raise your head a trifle and look at my forehead. I want to get the full

54

impact of your eyes. They're terrific." He blushed when Natalie laughed again, arranged lights, and then took several shots. "Now if I could have one of you standing beside your husband."

"Hey," Jack protested, "this is my wife's show. I'm not in this."

"Please, dear." She held out her hand.

"Sure." He drew her to her feet and, following the photographer's directions, they stood silhouetted against one of the long windows. The photographer knew his job. They were posed, facing each other, a picture, I felt, that should be used as the endpiece to *Prismed Light,* a perfect illustration of the married lovers.

As Natalie started back to her chair, the photographer said, "May I have one more? I'd like one of you with your daughter."

"My—" Natalie caught her breath.

"Constance," Jack said quickly, "is my wife's young niece. Amazing resemblance, isn't it? They might be sisters."

I shook my head. "I'm not dressed to have my picture taken. Anyhow, it's Natalie's story. I'd feel I was trying to horn in on her fame."

"Well, thanks a lot anyhow. This has been a privilege, Miss Netherfield." The photographer gathered up his equipment. As I started upstairs, I heard him say, "All right if I take the car, boss? I've got all this stuff to carry, and after the tree I'm covering the Burches' fiftieth wedding anniversary celebration at the other end of the village."

"Go ahead."

It must have been a couple of hours before Jack ushered out the local editor and the men from New York. In a few minutes Fowler and Tim came upstairs.

"Tired, darling?" Jack asked.

"Not really. But interviewers—I never know what to say. How can anyone explain how he writes poems? Or what drives him to do it, for that matter?"

"At least he spared you the one about your inspiration."

"That's one comfort. Though you'd hardly expect such silliness from a man in his position. How did it go, Jack? Did I make a fool of myself?"

"You! You were terrific as you always are, lovely and gracious, and that wonderful mind and spirit shining through those great eyes of yours. I'm glad the photographer had sense enough to appreciate your eyes. They're the first things I fell in love with; did I ever tell you that?"

"I've always wondered why."

"Suppose," he suggested, "I explain all the things I must have overlooked in the past year. There are hours before dinner. Darling!"

There was a silence and then they started up the stairs. I hastily pushed my door shut. It was intolerable that I should be spying on their lovemaking. At the door of their suite I heard her say, a catch in her voice, "He thought she —Constance—was my daughter. Jack, am I old?"

The door closed behind them and then another door shut softly, the door to Tim Struthers's room.

Six

Natalie was still wearing that stunning velvet housecoat when she came down to dinner, but that was not what made her appear so radiant. She wore the bloom of satisfied love, she seemed younger, and there was no trace of the weariness she had spoken of after her session with publisher, interviewers, and photographer.

Fowler said, "You know, Natalie, that young photographer hit the nail on the head. You do look the way one would expect a poetess to look."

"Poet," Jack corrected him solemnly. "The word poetess curdles my wife's blood."

"Well," she defended herself, "people don't say doctoress or lawyeress. And as for the word person—" Her vehemence made us all laugh.

"You're limping!" Fowler exclaimed.

"Just a blister on my heel. If you had any idea how many miles this man has made me walk—"

"Not with a blistered heel, I hope."

Jack laughed the gay, infectious laughter that was so irresistible. "It's much better now."

"How do you know?"

"Because it doesn't hurt me any more."

Fowler snorted in disgust, but I looked at Jack in surprise. Why, he really loves her, I thought. Oh, I'm glad. I'm glad.

That evening the cocktail time was gay, filled with light chatter about the wedding trip, the exotic and beautiful things they had seen, Natalie's daily increase in strength and endurance.

"He gave me the world," she said so simply that no one commented, but again I saw Tim's cold scrutiny of Jack, a look in which there was mingled a kind of perplexity with more than a suggestion of disbelief.

Fowler said abruptly, "I can't get over it. Seeing you sitting here instead of lying on a chaise longue in your little sitting room upstairs. And looking in that red garment, whatever it is," his hands made aimless fluttering gestures and everyone laughed, "like an American beauty rose."

All during dinner I was aware that Tim was attempting to catch my eye, but I refused to let him. The talk drifted idly. There was much to be said, but the time for anything important was not yet. That must wait until Natalie had gathered herself together and was prepared to resume her old life or begin a new one.

She was aware of this herself because she said, "Brendon, I know I've been treating you abominably when you have such a busy schedule and so many demands on your time. Tomorrow morning—not too early, perhaps ten-thirty— come up to my sitting room and we'll go over all the dreary business you like." She turned to Tim, smiling. "And on Monday we'll try to work out some sort of regular sched- ule. You'll have to explain to me how you prefer to work. I've never kept regular hours, of course. Poems aren't writ- ten that way. But I'll do my best to organize my thoughts and furbish up my memories—"

"I don't suppose," he said not quite unhopefully, "you've ever kept a diary."

"Why—I'm afraid not." Hearing the unconvincing note in her voice, she added, "There's never been anything much to record, as I've been warning you." She turned to me. "And we haven't yet had any real chance to talk, but we have all the time in the world, of course. There's so much I want to know about the little niece I've just discovered, and your poor mother—" She broke off. "No sad thoughts tonight, my dears. Let's do something quiet, unexciting, and normal: play bridge for an hour or two."

I shook my head. "I'm sorry. I don't know how." But for once I didn't even think of saying, "With the kind of life I've had, there was no opportunity to learn." My bitterness, so carefully nurtured, seemed to be dissolving fast.

"Then you can look on," Tim suggested, "and pick up at least the rudiments."

So for an hour and a half I sat behind Natalie's chair and watched the game, not very closely because cards didn't interest me. It was the people I found fascinating. Jack was engrossed in the game but I knew that, though he rarely looked at him, Tim had his attention fastened on him so intently that he played badly and the Cliffords, who were partners, won a notable victory.

When the game came to an end, Jack suggested highballs, which the men accepted, while Natalie said good night and went upstairs. Fowler appropriated the library and pulled out his pocket chessboard and the morning's chess problem. Tim came purposefully toward me, but I followed quickly on Natalie's heels.

For an hour I tossed restlessly, getting more and more wakeful. There was nothing to read. Tomorrow I'd buy a cheap FM radio so I could hear some music and, if Mr. Fowler ever vacated the library, I'd pick out some books. I heard footsteps on the stairs and assumed the men had gone to bed. At last I flung off the covers, got up and put on the larkspur taffeta dressing gown I had bought with Natalie's money. It was the most luxurious garment I had ever owned and I hadn't been able to resist it. I had not worn it before so I preened myself before the mirror, ran a comb through my hair, put on lipstick and powdered my nose. The robe was becoming but it had one drawback that I discovered when I started for the door. Though my satin slippers made no sound, the rich taffeta rustled with every step like crumpled paper.

There wasn't a sound in the house. I groped my way toward the stairs, past the closed doors, grasped the banister and went down cautiously because the robe was long and I did not want to trip and fall headlong. I reached the first floor and went into the library, groping for the light switch. So far, so good.

The bookshelves were beautifully arranged, and I worked my way from poetry to philosophy and history, past reference books and dictionaries, to essays and finally fiction. As I didn't want anything exciting, I hunted for something that would be soporific and found Fanny Burney's *Evelina*. I had almost reached the door when I heard the muffled voices and saw the dim light that seemed to come either from the short end of the dining room or from the butler's pantry beyond.

I started toward the library door but the rustling of the taffeta robe crackled like thunder in my ears and I stood still, my heart jumping erratically.

". . . piece of cake as our British friends say." That was Bates. I could hear the wheeze in his voice.

"No, there's a change of plans." That was a murmur.

"How come?" The wheeze was almost explosive.

If it occurred to me that I was developing an unattractive habit of eavesdropping, it did not distress me. I deliberately strained to hear every word.

"Let well enough alone."

"Delay is dangerous in these things. It makes me nervous. Stick to the original plan and let's get it over with." That was Bates again, Bates peremptory and insistent.

"The plans are changed. That is final."

"So you're sitting pretty, but how about me? I'm no pawn in your game, pal."

"You think that it's the other way?"

"I want action and I want it now."

There was a faint sound, near or far, I could not tell which, but I switched off the library light and stood pressed against the wall, shaking. *Let's get it over with.* Perhaps Alice had been right. Something evil was stirring in this beautiful house. *A nest of vipers.* And whatever was being planned, Bates was a part of it if not the active head.

Again I heard the faint sound, the harmless sound of ice tinkling against a glass, and Tim went past me, so close I could have touched him. I knew it was Tim because I could see him silhouetted against the window by the street light beyond.

And then he did an odd thing. He set down his glass on the hall table and bent over. When he stood up, I realized that he had removed his shoes. He went silently up the stairs. After his door closed, I followed as quietly as I could but when I reached the sanctuary of my own room I sank on the edge of the bed, shaking.

Tomorrow, I thought, I'd have to tell Brendon Fowler what I had overheard. Because something was wrong, horribly wrong, or that late-night meeting with its furtive talk would not have been necessary. Tim! Tim and Bates. Why had Tim come here? Why had he evaded all Mr. Fowler's attempts to find out what was behind his determination to come to this house for the ostensible purpose of writing a biography of Natalie?

I lay in the darkened room staring at the ceiling. I no longer thought of sleep but this was no time for *Evelina* either. Because something threatened Natalie, and I didn't know what to do about it.

Seven

At midmorning the lawyer had his promised talk with Natalie. The doors leading to the suite had been left open, by Alice, I suspected, as she was hovering close by in the hallway. I heard Fowler's voice raised in expostulation and then, as Tim started toward me purposefully, I went up to my room to put on the warm black coat I had purchased for a New England winter and, when I heard Tim in his own room, I ran down the stairs and made my escape. I didn't want to talk to him until I knew who and what he was and why he was really in Natalie's house, holding muffled conversations with her equivocal butler.

The sky was overcast but there was no rain and the temperature must have dropped fifteen degrees. I hugged the coat around me and wondered, as I walked briskly away from the green and toward the small shopping center, what was going to happen to me. Delightful as Natalie's house was, I felt like an intruder there. Whatever she expected of her unknown niece, it had not been a reminder of her youth. The photographer's unintentional blunder in referring to me as her daughter had come as an unwelcome surprise, a painful shock. No, I'd have to find some new way of life; someplace I could make my own and not be received on sufferance; some way of earning a living, which might be difficult, for times were hard, the list of the unemployed swelled from day to day, and I had no skill except as a typist.

But first, before I attempted to plan my own future, I had to decide what steps to take about Natalie. If I had been right and that midnight conversation had constituted a threat to her, someone must be warned. But should that someone be Natalie herself or Jack Clifford or Mr. Fowler?

I found a shop that sold radios and bought a small one with a surprisingly good tone. When I got back to the house, there was no one in sight except for a maid whom I had not seen before dusting the drawing room and removing the flower vases for fresh water. From the kitchen came the sound of the dishwasher and kettles being placed on the stove. Mrs. Bates was preparing for lunch. I wondered if she had any part in her husband's conspiracy—if there was a conspiracy.

Bates was raking up wet leaves, moving with all the animation of a stuffed doll. He wore thick work pants and a heavy sweater, with mittens and a stocking cap over his unengaging head.

The door of my room was open when I went up to deposit the little radio. Alice turned away from the dressing table with a guilty start and rushed into explanations. "I was just helping out because there's so much extra work with three guests. I made your bed and picked up the bathroom for you."

I looked at the photograph of Natalie she held in her hand and reluctantly she put it back on the stand for music scores. "Could be sisters," she said. "You aren't at all like your mother's side of the family, are you?"

"Do you remember my mother?"

"Of course I do; I'm not senile yet. Not that I saw much of her. When she wasn't up here practicing, she went on a concert tour. I guess the biggest surprise I ever had was

63

when she walked off with George Armstrong. Handsomest man I ever saw. Who'd ever have dreamed that he'd look at anyone but Miss Natalie, who was the beauty? I'll never figure out how Florence got him. Not a word to anyone. Just off in the night and a letter left behind."

"Thanks for doing my room, Alice. After this I can manage for myself."

"Guess you're used to that."

The insolence was so deliberate that I wondered whether Alice was trying to drive me out of the house—and why.

All this time the door of my room had stood open and now I could hear from the Cliffords' suite that Fowler was telling Natalie she carried her sense of duty to extremes.

"He oughtn't to worry her," Alice muttered.

"I'm pretty sure anything he did would be for her own good. He's an old friend, Alice, and a devoted one."

"Yes, only he doesn't know everything, way he thinks he does. But try to tell him and he just shrugs it off."

No, I thought, he hadn't shrugged off Alice's account of those two accidents, but perhaps he had ascribed them to the woman's corrosive jealousy.

"You planning to stay long?" she asked.

"I have no plans. There's really nothing more for you to do here, Alice. Thanks again."

She went out reluctantly, pausing as she passed me for a long look at my face. "Just the way she used to look, and the way she's always looked to me—until you came. I never noticed the change before. I guess she didn't either. We don't see ourselves grow older."

She went out as slowly as possible, paused in the hall and then darted into the lawyer's room. Another listening post. The bed had already been made and the room straightened. She hovered near the door.

Fowler's voice had risen. "That's nonsense, Natalie. You are really being absurd about this. A couple of accidents

that might have happened to anyone. You consult a for-
tuneteller—for God's sake!—and now you're letting yourself get almost into an hysterical state. You have everything: fame, beauty, a great talent, a devoted husband,
ample means, a healthy life. Remember those things and
drop this nonsense, this foolish and vicious suspicion
planted by a damned fool of a woman who can't bear to
have anyone near you but herself. If she could manage it,
she'd not only drive Clifford away but your niece as well.
A leech."

"Is that all it is, Brendon? Is that really all?" The lovely
voice was higher-pitched than I had ever heard it, touched
with hysteria. The lawyer had been right about that.

"Why don't you clear the air by talking frankly to Clifford about what Alice has been suggesting? If I don't miss
my guess, he'll dispose of it in one minute flat. And probably of her too."

"Oh, no, Brendon! I couldn't have that. She's been devoted to me for yeas."

"I'll grant you her devotion, but for my money she'd like
to keep you in cotton wool, put you back permanently on
that chaise longue with the door shut against people and
the windows closed against sunshine and life. Love can be
a great evil as well as a great good. The sooner you get rid
of the woman, the better. And clear the air, for God's sake,
by talking to Clifford."

"Oh, I can't. I can't. The very suggestion that I distrusted
him could destroy everything between us."

"What you're afraid to come out and say is that you half
believe Alice; you're letting her poisonous suggestions
weigh against a whole happy year with Clifford. You don't
trust your own husband. You're permitting that unbridled
imagination of yours to create horrors. Well, once before
you let that happen; you believed you had killed your
mother and you spent twenty years trying to appease the

angry gods." When she made no reply, he drove on relentlessly, "Why did you suddenly agree to have Struthers, a total stranger, come to this house? I'll tell you why. Not because you want the biography written but because you want someone here to protect you."

"Oh, no, no!" This time the lawyer did not break into her brooding. He waited. At length she spoke and the hysteria was gone, her voice was normal with some of the lovely warmth back again. "Jack thinks that young Struthers is interested in Constance. Do you?"

"I wouldn't be surprised. After all, they are both young."

"Young," she said broodingly.

"How long are you going to keep the girl here, Natalie?"

"It's her home, Brendon; the estate should have been divided equally between Florence and me. I'd like to make up to her—"

"One of your problems, Natalie, is that you are always trying to make a bargain with God." So he had paid attention to Tim. "It doesn't work, my dear."

"I wish you wouldn't talk in riddles."

"I'm trying to talk sense, but talking to you is like trying to grasp a handful of smoke. I suppose," Fowler added in resignation, "it's the poet in you. But there is one thing more."

"Brendon, I'm so tired. You've been at me and at me for hours."

"One hour and twenty minutes, to be exact. Have you discussed with your husband this drastic change in your will?"

"Yes, of course." She sounded surprised.

"How did he feel about it?"

"I don't think it mattered one way or another. He said he had enough to live on in comfort and to keep me too, if I didn't have my heart set on star sapphires and oceangoing yachts. He felt I should do as I thought best about my own estate."

"You didn't, either of you, think it rather excessive to make a fifty-fifty division with a girl you had never seen?"

"She is Florence's daughter and Florence has had—did have—a fairly rotten time of it, so far as I can make out. She sacrificed her own career for George and then he slipped down and down in degradation and there was nothing left but poverty and disgrace."

"Do you like Constance?"

"Like her? Of course I do. And she's so lovely to look at."

Fowler gave one of his rare laughs. "As you are so much alike you shouldn't say that. Self-praise. Well, I'll let you rest now, Natalie. I'll be driving back to New York after lunch. You'd better have a tray up here. You look done up. Sorry I've been such a trial to you. But remember I'm at your disposal whenever you need me, day or night. Always. But you know that."

"Brendon?" It was a startled question. "I—what a blind fool you must think me! I never realized you cared for me as a woman. I just thought of you as the best friend a woman ever had. Without you—"

"You aren't without me." There was only the faintest hint of bitterness in his voice. "Just try to keep on a steady keel, my dear. You're a happy woman. Stay that way. But don't—that is, you've given up all that nonsense about painkillers, haven't you?"

She laughed and it was a girl's laugh. "I have indeed. Jack hit the roof when he found I was in the habit of taking them. I told him nothing else had any effect on those horrible headaches. But he threw them all out and said all I needed was exercise and fresh air. So now I get blisters on my heels."

"Good," he said so fervently that they both laughed.

67

"Just the same, I do think it is absurd to suffer such pain because you refuse to wear glasses."

There was a hint of mischief in Natalie's voice as she said, "Tell me, Brendon, if you were a woman and had eyes like mine, would you wear glasses?"

"I give up. I'll never understand women. Good-bye, my dear."

Alice bustled out of the lawyer's room. "Oh, Mr. Fowler, I've just been making up your bed."

"Sorry to put you to all that work because you'll have to strip it again. I'm leaving this afternoon." He moved around in the next room, drawers opened and closed, a suitcase snapped shut. He was packing. Then, instead of turning toward the stairs, he came on to my room where I was kneeling, plugging the radio into the wall socket beside the bed. I turned it on, changing stations until I found WQXR and then I saw him standing in the doorway.

"May I come in?"

"Of course."

While I sat on the piano bench, he took the low rocking chair, which threw him off balance for a moment, but even in a rocking chair too small for him he managed to retain his dignity. He rested his bony hands on the chair arms, looked from the pretty four-poster bed to the small spinet to the open closet in which hung my new wardrobe. I hadn't noticed before that the door was open. Alice had certainly satisfied her curiosity. Then he looked at the open score on the spinet.

"Do you play?"

"Very little. We didn't have a piano after I was fifteen and then I would never have had my mother's talent."

"She was good. Very good. Music is practically my only hobby, or call it relaxation. But—that's odd, I'd never thought of it before—just as the real Natalie went into her poetry so the real Florence went into her music. The pian-

68

ist was a different person from the gentle, retiring, unassertive girl we knew." He added, "Or thought we knew," and I wondered why he, like Alice, had disliked my gentle mother.

"She didn't tinkle Chopin waltzes," he said. "She had a brilliant technique and a great deal of power and maturity. She was at her best in the big things, the later Beethoven sonatas, the Schumann *Fantasia in C.* And she could cope with most of the Chopin études. A pity, a great pity, that she should have given it all up."

"Well, she didn't have much choice. She loved my father and his work kept him in Hollywood. If she had gone on concert tours, she'd have been away seven or eight months a year. It wouldn't have worked as a marriage."

"And you think it worked better as it was?"

"Who can foresee the future? And somehow I can't blame my father for what happened; we loved him and he loved us. At home he was never the famous actor; he was just a delightful husband and father. We had an unlisted telephone to keep off intruders from our private life. He never—acted with us and that is why we were such a peaceful, happy family. I believe, as I've believed for years, that someone deliberately sabotaged his career."

"One thing you have in common with Natalie is an unbridled imagination."

I made no reply. There wasn't much I could say. After all, I had a completely unfounded suspicion, but I could remember, as the lawyer could not, what years of sliding downhill in his profession had done to my father, sapping his energy and finally his courage and hope. And he had tried. I could recall the nights when he had sat, clutching his head, trying in vain to memorize his lines; remember the night I had heard him crying, dreadful gasping sobs. Tears may be a relief to a woman, but pain like that could not be good for a man.

"Are you planning to take up a musical career?" Fowler asked.

I smiled at that. "At twenty? When I've done no practicing for five years and never had real talent, just a kind of facility, the sort of thing that often shows up in the young and leads to mistaken ideas of how much there is behind it?"

"Then what?"

"I don't know."

"You're only twenty and you have exceptional looks, as you must be aware. I wonder that Hollywood studio didn't want to make an actress of you instead of a typist."

"Oh, they did, but I'm not photogenic." It was easier to lie than to try to explain that I couldn't bear to attempt to grasp my father's mantle. He had been as generous as any man could be, but it would have hurt to be replaced, supplanted, by his own daughter. I had never told even my mother of the director's insistence about making a screen test and his exasperation when I refused so much as a walk-on part.

The lawyer settled himself in an attempt to be comfortable in the little rocking chair, but he gave no indication of leaving. "Well, now, let's put our heads together," he said, with an attempt at bonhomie that wouldn't have fooled a backward ten-year-old. "There's nothing in Alcott to interest or stimulate a young girl. A little more than two hours away by bus there is New York with all its glitter and excitement, the best music in the world, music to choose from every night in the year, and more things to do than you have ever dreamed of, lots of them still cheap, believe it or not.

"Why don't you give yourself a week or so with your aunt, so you can get to know each other, and then come down to New York? I could fit you easily into our typing pool and you'd earn enough to have a one-room apartment

70

and something left over for food and fun."

I asked bluntly, "Is that what Aunt Natalie wants?"

He was taken aback, almost flustered. "Of course not. Nonsense. What gave you such an idea?"

"You did."

For once he was thrown off balance, fumbling for words.

"I wish you'd tell me the truth, Mr. Fowler. I don't know my aunt. Would it be like her to make a tremendous gesture and send for me, ask me to make my permanent home here, and then, the next moment, change her mind and want to turn me out? It's important for me to know. How temperamental is she?"

He seized on the word almost gratefully. "Temperamental? Well, of course, I suppose all real artists are. And occasionally moody. But that doesn't mean anything. And she is so completely happy now in her married life that I doubt that she will ever again be subject to moods. They grew out of that long invalidism, you know, when her emotional energies had no other outlet. All she needs is love and reassurance, and Clifford gives her that. At least—he seems to."

"Oh, he really loves her," I assured him confidently. "I don't judge by the big reassuring words but the little things. Like—well, when he said he knew her heel was better because it didn't hurt him any more. That was real."

"She must be able to go on believing that, Constance." Fowler used my name for the first time. "She needs reassurance. Any doubts—"

I must be unusually slow in reacting. Nearly a minute passed before I said blankly, "You can't possibly think I'd try to interest Jack Clifford? It's preposterous."

"You may not have noticed it, but when he laughs you laugh."

"Well, anyone would."

"Struthers didn't. I didn't."

I couldn't say: You are eaten up with jealousy of the man. In fact, I couldn't say anything.

The interview obviously had not gone as he had intended. He pulled himself up with some difficulty out of the little chair, drew a card from his pocket and scrawled on it. "This will give you my phone numbers both at the office and at home. After southern California you are going to find New England winters difficult to cope with. Beautiful, of course, but often there is savage cold and after a real storm you might be housebound for days. What seems pleasant to you now might well become a prison."

I thought of the furnished room where my mother and I had lived those last months. I thought of the men who assumed an unattached girl in Hollywood was legitimate prey and who turned any date into a wrestling match. I thought of the comfort and security of this house. I said, "Thank you, Mr. Fowler."

"Think about what I have said. New York has more to offer you than you could imagine, and a fuller life on your own than you could have here in your aunt's shadow."

On that he went out of the room and down the long curving staircase. I heard him speak to Jack Clifford, who had just come in and was closing the front door. "Getting a little exercise?"

"I tried to give Bates a hand with the leaves, but it's no use. One thing sure; he isn't built for outdoor work."

Like a blow over the heart I remembered that Mr. Fowler had so surprised me by his attempts to lure me away from the house that I had forgotten altogether to tell him about the sinister overtones of the conversation I had overheard the night before.

"Or indoor work so far as I can tell," Fowler said. "Where on earth did you rake him up?"

"Agency."

"What agency? I'd like to know which one to avoid."

Clifford laughed. "Well, these days we take what we can get. It could be worse."

"I don't know how."

"He might have epileptic fits. Anyhow, his wife can cook and that's no small blessing."

"I'm with you there." The lawyer went into the library and, uncharacteristically, closed the door.

I wandered around my room and then resolutely tackled the third Chopin prelude, playing the left hand in whole notes, half notes, quarter notes. Some of the stiffness and weakness was going out of my fingers, but my wrists and shoulders were rigid. For a change I went back to the Schubert. I wasn't ready yet for the discipline of scales and exercises—who said that Czerny hated little children?—I was just feeling my way. But you can't practice if you do it mechanically, letting your fingers do your thinking for you, and I was thinking about Mr. Fowler's curious insistence on my leaving Alcott. In some way he believed I constituted a threat to Natalie's happiness.

After I closed the spinet, I settled down with *Evelina,* not wanting to risk any conversation with Jack Clifford that would stir Mr. Fowler's suspicion. Fanny Burney's romantic novel might serve as a sedative, but it wasn't much help in catching and holding a restless mind. From Tim Struthers's room came a sudden barrage of sound as he tackled his typewriter at furious speed.

Eight

Natalie did not come down for lunch.

"My wife tells me you are going back to New York this afternoon," Jack Clifford said.

Fowler nodded. "The work piles up and I've had to postpone some appointments."

"It was good of you to come. I know Natalie appreciated it. You provide her with a kind of—I guess the word is support—that she needs. And I'm glad on my own account that you were able to give us a few days. In the past we've hardly said more than hail and farewell."

"Natalie has been a dear friend for a long time and I had a feeling of extra responsibility because her sister dropped out of her life and she lost both her parents. She was helpless in many ways, not merely because of her precarious health but her utter lack of practical business sense, which, of course, makes her—vulnerable."

There was a look of amused comprehension on Jack Clifford's face. He was as quick as a cat at grasping undercurrents. "I don't really know," he said, "why we should beat about the bush, unless it's an occupational hazard for a lawyer. What you'd really like to know—and there's no reason on earth why you shouldn't—is how well fixed I am financially and whether I'm going to become a pensioner of Natalie's, taking unfair advantage of her utter lack of practical business sense."

He brushed aside the lawyer's somewhat flustered protests. "I don't blame you. Things look bad for me." Again amusement quirked his lips. "I toil not, neither do I spin. Like that feckless but enviable character in Housman: 'About the woodlands I will go/To see the cherry hung with snow.' "

Fowler's expression made me choke and I grasped for my napkin to cover the grin I could not repress. Tim, graven-faced, thrust a glass of water into my hand, which nearly undid me.

"The thing is," Jack said, "I have enough money for the things I enjoy doing. No extravagant tastes. There's no pressing need to go into the marketplace just because everyone else does. Life's too short for all the living and experiencing I want to do, for all the looking and thinking. 'What is this life if, full of care,/We have no time to stop and stare?' "

This time it was Fowler who choked and, in an unwary moment, I met Tim's dancing eyes.

"Sorry," Jack said blandly, "I seem to have picked up a taste for poetry from Natalie and by now it comes natural. All I'm trying to say is that I just don't give a damn about my wife's money. So far as dividing her estate with Constance is concerned, I'm all for it. I can't think of a nicer person to have it. So I hope that takes some of the intolerable burden off your shoulders."

This time it was Bates, passing his wife's flaky muffins, who had a fit of coughing until he was red in the face and retired in confusion through the swing door of the butler's pantry.

Later, as Bates was bringing down Fowler's suitcase and turning it over to Fowler's taciturn chauffeur, Natalie made a brief appearance.

She held out both hands. "Brendon dear—thank you again for everything."

He shook hands briskly with the two men and turned to me. "Then I'll expect to see you in a couple of weeks, Constance. Give me a ring when you arrive." Having disposed of my plans in his own inimitable manner, without waiting for my approval, he took his leave.

Natalie smiled at me. "We still haven't had a real talk, have we? Perhaps tomorrow. Brendon is the Rock of Gibraltar, but he does tire me. Why don't you and Mr. Struthers—oh, I am going to call you Timothy—take the car and do some exploring? There are such pretty drives around here, even after the foliage is gone. Or do you want the car, darling?"

"No," Jack said. "Believe it or not, I'm going to catch up on some bills and letters. Something," and he smiled at her, "seems to have distracted my attention lately." He grinned, the grin growing to a chuckle. "I feel I owe it to Mr. Fowler to display some industry. Anyhow, it's time we let the kids go off on their own."

"Come on, Kate," Tim said.

"Kate?" Jack asked in surprise.

"She's a shrew. Hadn't you noticed?"

"A beautiful girl is wasted on you," Jack declared. "Can't you do better than this guy, Constance?"

"Heavens, I hope so."

When we were in the car, Tim switched on the heater. "Mind if I smoke?"

I shook my head.

"I've given up cigarettes and I'm cultivating a pipe. When I'm famous I'll be ready to pose with a pipe clutched in my fist. It's expected, you know. You grasp the stem and look into space in a brooding way as though thinking deep thoughts."

"Wouldn't that be a strain on you?"

He ignored that, filling and lighting his pipe. "What was all that talk about you going to New York?"

"It was Mr. Fowler's idea. He suggested a job in his office. He's trying to be kind to me on Natalie's account."

"That's what I figured, but not the way you mean it. You're stiff competition, gal, and what's more, you're what she has seen herself as being all these years. When she got close enough to take a good look at you she was stunned, and when that photographer thought you were her daughter, it was a body blow."

"You're wrong. Mr. Fowler says New York is more stimulating, that there is nothing here to interest me."

"No?" Tim asked provocatively.

"Definitely no," I assured him.

"Now, Kate," he began cajolingly.

"And if you weren't impossible in every other way," I said indignantly, "handing me that glass of water at lunch—"

"I figured you'd need it. Did you get a good look at Fowler when Clifford said, 'About the woodlands I will go/To see the cherry hung with snow'?' I thought the poor devil was going to be sick then and there—and at the lunch table too."

"Even Bates choked."

"That was what is known as a horse laugh."

I began to laugh helplessly, all the laughter that had been bottled up at lunch. "What do you suppose made Jack do it?"

"Sheer deviltry and the fun of getting Fowler's goat. All that talk about his finances—"

"But Mr. Fowler didn't ask. Jack volunteered the information."

"He did, didn't he? Still you could see Fowler was simply seething with curiosity and suspicion."

"Suspicion?"

"You really bristle at any oblique attack on the engaging Mr. Clifford, don't you? Let us approach this matter in a spirit of detachment. Leave us take a squint at the facts. Now here we have a middle-aged woman with an income of at least fifty thousand a year—just income, mind you—swept off her feet by a guy twelve years younger than she, a guy who is darned attractive to women."

"How would you know?"

"I watched your reactions," Tim said coolly.

"You—"

"Count to ten in fractions. It helps," he said kindly.

"But you have no right—anyone can see that he's devoted to Natalie, that he makes her happy, that he doesn't care about her money. He said himself that he has enough for his needs."

"His simple needs. Yeah, I heard him."

"If you're so damned suspicious and such a marvel at solving crimes that better men have failed at—"

"Ouch!"

"Why don't you find out for yourself where Jack's money comes from?"

"Oh, I know where it comes from."

"You mean," I was almost sputtering, "you actually checked on him before you came here?"

"I actually did. In fact—"

"Why are you really here?"

When he made no reply, I said, "I'll bet Jack inherited his money."

"Right the first time. He inherited it."

"Well, then!"

"But not from his family. No trace of a family anywhere. From an elderly woman, a wealthy woman named Evans, Gertrude Evans. She got herself killed by a hit-run driver and it turned out she had recently changed her will, cutting out her only living relative, a nephew named Hugh Evans, and left the works to Mr. Jack Clifford, who doesn't care about money."

"What you are suggesting is monstrous."

"My, what a big word for such a little girl. Look here, Kate—"

"Don't call me that!"

"I can think of other names I'd rather call you, but I don't like rushing things. Anyhow, while you are all starry-eyed about Clifford—"

"That's a lie!"

"Mustn't be rude. Now honestly, Kate, before you blow up again, did you fall for all that stuff about tiptoeing through the tulips?"

"Yes, I did. Oh, not literally, of course. He was just having a little fun at Mr. Fowler's expense. Mr. Fowler does ask for it; he's so pompous."

Tim relit his pipe, practically turning the action into a ritual. He pushed back that recalcitrant lock of hair and turned to give me a quick look before he speeded up the car. It was an unexpectedly sober look.

"I'll give you pompous but Fowler is no fool. Far from it. He can smell a rat in the wall as fast as the next man."

"Tim!" I hesitated for a long time.

"Yes?" he said more gently than I'd heard him speak. "Get it off your mind, kid."

"Your window was open too when Alice talked to Mr. Fowler about the accidents."

"It was open."

"Did you—could you honestly believe that Jack Clifford engineered two attempts to murder Natalie—and on her honeymoon, too?"

"Well, there were the brides in the bath. No, I'm not trying to be funny. I honestly don't know. And by this time there is no possible way of finding out the truth. Either one could have been what it appeared to be, sheer accident: the ptomaine poisoning, the fall off the cliff. Only—"

"Well?"

"Well, there was a lot at stake. Not just the income, but the house and furnishings. Museum stuff so far as I can tell. And those paintings in the drawing room are originals, worth tens of thousands at least. And then," he puffed at his pipe, dropping speed. Like all good drivers, he instinctively lowered speed when he was preoccupied. "And then there was Gertrude Evans. She was run down at a most opportune moment. There's no evidence, no witness to the car that struck her. But Jack Clifford made over two hundred thousand out of that deal, while the nephew got one measly thousand. A token. And there's no reason to think the Evans woman was the first victim. It was too smooth an operation. Up to now our engaging and plausible Mr. Clifford has done damned well for himself without going, as he puts it, into the marketplace. He's only twenty-eight, with a bright future ahead, free to tiptoe through the tulips to his heart's content."

"I don't believe it," I said at last.

"But, my dear girl, I know the whole story of that Evans deal. That's what put me onto Clifford in the first place. The nephew was a classmate of mine at Brown. He told me about it because I'd done those books on unsolved murders. He thought I might try my hand at this. Because, my dear, for what it is worth, Hugh not only believes Clifford conned his aunt out of her money but that he was the one who ran her down."

When I made no comment, he said, gently mocking, "Still doubting Thomasina?"

"I don't know about the Evans case, of course. Perhaps she did like Jack better than her nephew or perhaps she had some reason for disliking her nephew. After all, relatives quite often do dislike each other."

"How true that is!"

"But I don't think Jack would kill anyone. And I honestly believe he is devoted to Natalie, tremendously proud of her, and he feels humble about the great love she has given him."

"Well, well!"

I reminded him of Jack's comment about the blister on his wife's heel. "No one would have thought that way if he hadn't loved her."

"Ha, ha," Tim said flatly.

"But—"

"We have been sent out to get better acquainted, in the hope that a beautiful friendship will ripen between us."

"Ha, ha," I echoed his mirthless ejaculation.

"And to bring about this consummation devoutly to be wished, let us now leave the dubious past of Mr. Clifford and the dubious future of Mrs. Clifford—"

"Don't joke about it!"

"All right. We are now going to talk about you. For instance, why, with your looks, were you a typist in the studio where your father had worked?"

"I don't want to be an actress." I didn't expatiate.

"You know, Kate, you must be unique."

"Do you think every girl yearns to act?"

"A beautiful girl who not only does not exploit her looks but practically ignores them—"

"If you can't talk about anything else—"

"Okay. Okay. To hear is to obey. Temporarily, at least. But I wonder if Fowler is right in thinking you'd be better off alone in New York. You have about as much ability to protect yourself in the clinches as you have to fly."

"Considering that I've been supporting myself since I was sixteen and that I nursed my mother for two years without help from anyone, I think I can look after myself fairly well."

He shifted the subject abruptly. "Tell me about your mother. Was she like her sister?"

"Not a bit. She took after her mother's side of the family,

smaller than Natalie, with light fluffy hair and mild blue eyes and a kind of gentleness. It was only when she played the piano that she displayed such tremendous power and a brilliant technique. But away from the piano she was almost timid; there was no fight in her. I think her mother must have been like that too, but her father was a violent man. He crushed both his daughters as well as his wife."

"At least your mother got away."

"Yes, and in spite of the tragedy of those last years she was happy. I think she would have voted that it had been worth all the suffering."

"From what I've seen on the late, late shows your father was a man who could have swept any woman off her feet."

"But he didn't. I mean he didn't play around with other women. He loved my mother just because she wasn't like the ones who were always trying to attract him by their glamour. She wasn't a bit glamorous. She was just—sweet. But not cloying."

"He was happy in his marriage, he was tops in his career, but he—fell apart. Why?"

"I don't know. The studios stopped giving him big roles while his rating was still high. It was only after things got so bad that he started to drink."

"But that was a result, not a cause. Could anyone have been deliberately sabotaging him?"

I turned to him eagerly. "You know you're the first person who ever suggested that. I thought I was the only one. When I said it to Mr. Fowler, he told me I had an unbridled imagination."

"Did he indeed?" Tim sounded interested and I was belatedly aware of how much information he had been getting out of me. He asked almost idly, "Where is your father now?"

I turned at bay. "I'm surprised you haven't checked up on him."

"I have," he said coolly. "I always research my jobs as thoroughly as I can, including the byways and the side paths. You never know where they'll lead or when someone will drop a hint that takes you in a new direction."

"Have I done that?" I asked suspiciously.

"No, but Alice did."

"What was that?"

"Figure it out for yourself. You heard her. But somehow I believe your father is around somewhere. He was too famous to die without leaving a trace; too well known, however much he may have changed. If there was some way of getting word to him of your present prosperity, it might smoke him out."

"I'll never forgive you for that."

"Oh, yes, you will."

"Take me home."

"She said through gritted teeth."

I literally did grind them in my fury and Tim laughed aloud. "Oh, Kate! Darling Kate! It's so easy to get a rise out of you that it isn't even sporting."

"I didn't realize that sportsmanship was one of your attributes. And just what were you talking about to Bates in the butler's pantry—yes, we're going to talk about you for a change. And what did he mean when he said: 'Let's get it over with'?"

"How in hell—" he began, startled.

"And you were careful to take off your shoes before you sneaked upstairs."

"You'd better get down to New York on the first bus. Or I'll take you down myself if I have to drag you. It isn't safe to stick your pretty little nose into matters that don't concern you. It just might get caught in a trap."

I made no reply. He knocked out his pipe and put it on the dashboard. "Now I wonder," he said, more as though he were talking to himself, "if that's why Fowler wanted to get you away from here. That's a grim thought. The more I see the possibilities in this case ramifying, the less I like it. It isn't simply your curiosity that is dangerous, but there are other factors. Natalie isn't the only one who is threatened. There's a girl who stands to take half the Netherfield estate and who could be very, very much in someone's way."

I didn't speak.

"Okay," he said at last, "if you've got to dig into this unsavory mess, I'll explain. Believe it or not, I wasn't talking to Bates or to anyone else. I went down to fix myself a nightcap from that bar in the small end of the L. That interesting conversation took place between Bates and Clifford who, apparently, had never met before. It makes you think, doesn't it?"

"So, after all, you are really working at your old job, trying to solve old murders."

"Or prevent new ones."

Nine

If Tim was to be believed, not only Natalie but I too was in danger. If Tim was to be believed. That took a lot of getting used to.

"You came here," I said at last, "because your friend Hugh Evans says Jack Clifford not only conned his aunt out of her money but probably was responsible for her death as well. So he put you on Jack Clifford's trace, persuaded you to get some sort of pipeline into the house, which you did by pressuring Natalie into letting you write her biography. You checked up not only on Jack but on Natalie and me and my father. Why?"

"I had to know the score. Try to understand that, Kate. I wasn't completely sold on the idea of Clifford as a killer, though I was sold on his being a con man who preyed on wealthy women, and if I'd had any doubts, they'd have cleared up in the first hour after meeting him. He's no amateur at the job. Smooth as silk. He plays the part of a big, honest guy humbled by the great love of his famous and once beautiful wife; a simple guy, clear as glass, not striving in the marketplace, just tiptoeing through the tulips."

"Oh, I wish you'd stop saying that!"

"Okay. Order received and contents noted. But then I overheard Alice tell Fowler about those two 'accidents.' Now, wait," as I started to interrupt, "they may be, probably were, just what they appeared to be. Clifford is no fool. It's a familiar situation: young husband, wealthy middle-aged wife. The police might wonder. They might probe back and discover the untimely demise of Gertrude Evans. Too damned risky.

"In the second place, I can see as well as you can that Alice is corroded with jealousy, that she regards Natalie as her own special property and resents having anyone near her. And that includes you, my trusting friend. Then I overhear a very interesting and furtive confabulation between Clifford and Bates—and if Bates was ever a house-man before, I'll eat my hat."

"His wife is a good cook."

"What that has to do with it, my straw-headed darling, I can't imagine. I'd place Bates as the kind who passes hot tips at the race track, who keeps tabs on the women who appear in expensive jewelry and finds out where they live, who finds likely prospects for his confederate, and then leaves Clifford to weave his spell. And I can't believe Gertrude Evans was the first victim. He worked that will change in a little over three months, won her confidence by claiming to represent a group raising funds for handi-capped children. It's curious how many otherwise hard-headed people will fall for any so-called charity if the ap-peal is on an impressive letterhead and has a name of important sponsors. They don't check it out.

"Well, Clifford got Miss Evans interested, and began to drop in more and more often as they discovered mutual interests. That is one of his specialties, like stuffing himself with poetry until it comes out of his pores to please Nata-lie."

"How you hate him!"

"I don't like leeches, but, on the whole, I take my hat off to the guy. He's good at his job. Very good. But now he seems to be at the parting of the ways with his confederate and when thieves fall out there is trouble brewing. Plenty of trouble. From what I—we," and he grinned at me, "overheard, Bates wants to get on with the original plan and Clifford has changed his mind. Now here," he said in a pontifical manner, "we enter the field of speculation."

"I didn't know we'd ever left it."

"You really are a little shrew," Tim said amiably. "My own feeling is that Bates expected Natalie to be disposed of on the wedding trip, once she had made her will. I think he came here to keep Clifford to the point. He wants the job done without delay. From his standpoint there's nothing to be gained by waiting. But—and here's the catch. Unknown to Bates, Natalie has had a strong attack of guilty conscience and has decided to divide her estate between her husband and a niece who had a raw deal. The said niece presents an obstacle. As long as she is alive and kicking— and she kicks very well—it's better to bide their time. That's the message I think Clifford was trying to put across, and that is why I think you'd be a very smart little girl to get the hell out of here and accept Fowler's offer. Don't take too long making up your mind. I can't watch you day and night. That is, I have no personal objection, but there might be some awkwardness about it."

"I'm sure you could think of a convincing reason," I said sweetly.

"The yearning I have to turn you over my knee and wallop the bejasus out of you is almost more than I can withstand."

"Let's go back home," I said, and knew my voice was shaking.

"I have a better idea, a lot of better ideas, but I'll creep up on them gradually." He laughed like a villain in an old melodrama. "Let's go up the pike a couple of miles to a place where they make a terrific hot rum punch, cinnamon and spices and no blasphemy like melted butter."

"Didn't take you long to find a place like that." Some of my spirit came back.

He grinned. "Well, I got the cold shoulder and went out in search of comfort. Come on. We can be back at the house in an hour and some of that frozen feeling will be gone. I guarantee it."

I didn't deny the frozen feeling. To have someone tell you quite calmly that your life is threatened, that it can be ended at any minute in some unexpected way: a blow on the head, poisoned food, a fall, a hit-run driver—I shivered.

The steaming hot rum punch, the glass carefully wrapped in a napkin, thawed out some of the chill, but Tim helped most. He seemed to have forgotten the ugly specters he had conjured up and instead made me laugh in spite of myself by a series of ridiculous and undoubtedly apocryphal stories of his boyhood and family. By the time he had parked the car in the big garage and Bates admitted us, we were both laughing and relaxed. I could even see Bates without trying to stare at him, wondering what sort of man he was. I could eat dinner without listening to every word Clifford said, trying to find some hidden meaning.

After dinner Natalie began to make plans. She and Tim were to spend two hours a morning in conversation, from ten-thirty to twelve-thirty. People ran dry after that, Tim insisted. The freshness was gone. And there wouldn't be a deadly question-and-answer procedure, but a kind of relaxed free association. Then he'd spend a part of every afternoon putting his notes in order.

"And of course I have that book of reviews and criticisms and a copy of the speech you made when you accepted the Pulitzer award. They will give me a kind of warming-up exercise."

For the fifth time since we had sat down at dinner, Bates came in to announce a telephone call. Natalie laughed ruefully.

"Please don't make me tell you this every time, Bates. I want you to get the names of people who call, take down messages, if any, and tell everyone—*everyone*—that I am recuperating from my trip and cannot accept any telephone calls."

"Have you got that?" Jack demanded.

"Yes, sir."

I'd been doing a lot of hard thinking. When I tried to be cool and logical, I thought Tim's whole point of view was ridiculous. The rest of the time I remembered that muffled conversation, remembered Alice's somewhat overwrought talk with Fowler. One thing I had to accept. Jack and Joe Bates were not strangers. Like it or not, that much had to be admitted. But what worried me most was Natalie. She'd had so much unhappiness and if I were to take my suspicions to her, if they were suspicions, I could wreck that precarious happiness. But if I said nothing and something happened to Natalie—

I crumbled a roll on my butter plate. If there was a conspiracy, I was the stumbling block. Until I had been disposed of, she should be safe enough. So I'd have to stay here until I was sure, one way or the other, because my existence was the only real safeguard she had. They had to get me first.

The queer thing is that I wasn't afraid. Down in my heart I couldn't believe any of it. Alice was jealous of being edged out of first place at Natalie's side. Tim was trained to look for mysteries—oh, all right, unsolved murders. But still he had a writer's imagination and he could easily be spinning a tale out of nothing at all for the sheer intellectual excitement of it. And nothing could shake my belief that, whatever he might have done in the past, Jack was genuinely devoted to his wife.

"Look," I said suddenly, making Natalie start. "Oh, sorry, I didn't mean to be so abrupt, but it just occurred to me. I haven't a single thing to do. Why can't I at least handle the telephone calls for you and stave off people until you are ready to talk to them?"

"Thank God for Constance!" Jack said fervently.

Tim gave me a long sober look.

"It's wonderful of you," Natalie said, "but the trouble with making such an offer is that people take advantage. I know you can type and there are bundles and bundles of letters on my desk, some of which have been waiting for weeks. I lie awake thinking of them. Would you—but it is taking advantage—"

"If you'd give me an idea of what you want to say, I could answer them for you, using Tim's typewriter while he works with you in the mornings."

"You wouldn't mind?"

"I'd like having something to do. Honestly."

"Don't," Jack advised his wife, "look a gift horse in the mouth."

Natalie laughed. "Of all the ungracious things to say! My dear, you'd take a terrific load off my mind. To me those letters seem as high as a mountain, and as for the telephone—"

"Good. That's all settled then."

After dinner, Natalie and Jack settled down to a game of gin rummy and Tim went up to his room to do some preliminary work. I excused myself and went into the library for something more stimulating than *Evelina*, found Catherine Drinker Bowen's *Miracle at Philadelphia*, which I'd wanted to reread when there was time, and Mary Webb's *Precious Bane*, still one of the most beautiful novels I knew, and went up to settle myself in the rocking chair, and switched on the radio.

In a moment of aberration someone at the station had put on Tchaikovsky's *1812 Overture*, so I shut it off hastily and settled down with Mrs. Bowen. It was good to remember now, two hundred years later, how a handful of men, some of them still in their twenties, none of them sharing the same point of view, had shaped the framework of a new nation and a new way of life by integrity, by compromise, by common sense, perhaps by genius. When I switched out my light, I had the feeling of comfort one gets from the company of men of high purpose and courage.

II

Alice brought me a note from Natalie while I was still at breakfast. "Why don't you come up when you've finished and I'll turn over this awful mass of letters to you and we'll discuss what to do with them. You're really an angel to do this. I never meant to put you to work. Love, Natalie."

This morning she was in the sitting room between the two bedrooms, wearing another lavish housecoat, this one a peach-colored velvet, with long wide sleeves and a mandarin collar. Again she wore her hair as I did mine.

She held out both hands when I went in, and drew me down to brush her cheek against mine. She pointed in dismay at the stacks of letters on the table and the floor beside her. She hadn't, she confessed, even opened them.

"If you'd go through them—there won't be anything personal, so you needn't hesitate—and put them in separate piles, you'll find some of them need only a brief note of acknowledgment and thanks." She reached for an ornate case and drew out a thin steel stiletto with a magnificent sapphire on the end. It was a perfect thing. "Jack got it for me in Toledo and I use it as a letter opener. It came from the strangest curio shop that handled pieces hundreds of years old that had come from once wealthy families. The sapphire is so perfect I chose this. It will make your work more pleasant."

I shook my head. "I'd be terrified of something happening to it."

As I began turning over the piles of letters idly, she said, "You can tell some of them that as soon as I have the time and energy I'll answer them personally. Do whatever seems best to you. And there's no rush. Some of them have been here a long time. For weeks and weeks we wouldn't have a forwarding address. We just went where our fancy took us," and her face wore the glow it always did when she was thinking of her husband.

I started to gather them up and they kept tumbling out of my arms. Natalie laughed and indicated a small, ornate wastebasket beside her chair. "Dump them in that," she suggested, and I did so, while she fingered an odd ornament hanging on a silver chain around her neck.

"My lucky piece," she said. "In his first letter Jack sent me a four-leaf clover he had found and, because it seemed like an omen, I had it covered with plastic to preserve it. I always have it with me. Always. Not obviously, of course, but in my pocket or in my bra. The day it came I had the strangest feeling that it brought me life. I feel now that to lose it would bring me death."

"Oh, don't!" I expostulated, shocked.

"Don't you ever have premonitions?"

I shook my head.

"Lucky you," Natalie said lightly. "Lately I've had a recurrent dream." She broke off. "Do you remember your dreams?"

"Sometimes, in snatches, but they never make sense."

"I keep dreaming of a knife," Natalie said somberly. "Over and over."

"I'm glad you'll be settling down to work," I said matter-of-factly. "Get your mind on something sensible."

She laughed at that. "You are going to be good for me, so practical and so down-to-earth."

92

Before I could leave the room, she checked me. "Oh, don't go now. Tim and I won't be working for another hour and we haven't talked at all. There's so much I want to know. All those years and no word. Tell me about Florence. Was she dreadfully unhappy?"

"Well, of course, she was very ill those last months and a lot of the time she was sedated so the pain, at least, was under control and she wasn't too keenly aware of her condition." I found to my surprise and relief that I could talk of her now without bitterness, without anger toward Natalie and the Netherfields. No one, after all, had been to blame. I suppose it is a human instinct to seek for a scapegoat.

"And before that? Poor darling, with that disastrous marriage! It was doomed to failure from the start. If she had only confided in her family! But she just slipped off with George and not a word to anyone. Poor Florence just wasn't his type."

"Actually, she was. There were always women chasing him, and Hollywood, especially then, simply oozed pretty women on the prowl. But Mother was gentle and sweet and he loved her for that. Even in Hollywood with its ruthless gossip commentators, there was never a breath of scandal about my father and other women. Oh, of course, later—"

"That's when he began to drink?" Natalie's voice was gentle. "Of course we heard about that. He just faded out, didn't he?"

"I think he was more or less pushed out." I could hear the defiance in my voice. "I realize no one agrees with me, but the drinking came only after the studios had practically closed their doors on him. He couldn't understand it. He tried desperately, and Mother never lost faith in him. She went right on loving him and believing in him, even when the drinking got hold of him and he began to change. But he never changed toward her. He just—when he knew that

93

he was finished and a burden—he just went away. He was not running away from us; he was trying to spare us."

"And you don't know what happened to him?"

"I saw him on the street once in Beverly Hills, once in Hollywood, and once in Los Angeles. I didn't speak because I knew he would have hated to have me see him like that, shabby and defeated and unshaven. And once I saw him staggering. He was very drunk. That was about four years ago. The last time."

"Have you tried AA and the shelters they have for people of that kind?"

I shook my head. "If he had wanted to be found, he would have let us know."

"Poor George. Poor Florence. Such tragic waste." Natalie put her small hand on mine. "We'll make the future so bright for you that you can forget those sad things. But what did Brendon mean about you going to New York?"

"He was good enough to offer me a job if I couldn't find a way of keeping busy here."

"How very kind of him!"

"Wasn't it?"

"But you do understand, don't you, that there's no further need for you to earn money? I hate all these sordid business details, but Brendon will explain to you that you're to have a regular income."

This was the time to say that I wished she would change her will and not divide the estate between Jack and me. But if I did that there would be nothing to stop Bates, at least, from attempting to remove Natalie. Remove! What a mealy-mouthed word for murder.

All this time Alice had been deliberately hovering in Natalie's bedroom, ostensibly hanging up clothes and straightening the dressing table, but listening to what was being said. She spoke now, "There's the telephone again.

Poor Mr. Clifford is being kept busy."

"Heavens, I forgot that was my job now." I ran down the stairs. Jack was just turning away from the telephone.

"One invitation for Natalie to speak at a Book and Author luncheon; one call urging her to attend a reception in her honor; one call from a neighbor whom she hasn't seen for years, offering to do anything she can at any time for dear, dear Natalie."

I laughed. "Sorry I reneged on the job. I've just been collecting Natalie's mail. It looks like the Christmas rush at the General Post Office."

"Thank you, Constance. This will be a big load off her mind. It's been rather worrying her. She has gained so much that I don't want her to lose any of it by taking on too much at first. Anyhow, her mind should be left free for her poetry."

"Of course it should and I'm glad to have something to do. Anyhow it's a lot more interesting working for a poetess—"

"Poet." He grinned.

"—than sending out form letters saying 'Your photograph and résumé are on file and we'll inform you when we are doing any casting.' "

The phone rang and I went to answer it. The man at the other end of the line wanted Natalie. He was insistent about it even when I told him as firmly as I could that Mrs. Clifford was taking no calls at present. If he cared to leave a message—

"Grace," he said. "The name is Grace. Howard Grace. She'll know. Tell her it's important. Time is of the essence."

"I'll tell her, Mr. Grace." I hung up and turned, frowning, to Jack.

"Anything wrong?" he asked quickly.

"I don't think so. Just an awfully persistent man. The kind who won't take no. She's to call him because time is of the essence."

"And who is this general nuisance?"

"His name is Grace. Howard Grace."

"He probably sells insurance. No use bothering Natalie about it."

I went upstairs but, though Jack had said not to bother, something about the telephone call disturbed me. I reported it to Natalie. "Jack didn't want me to bother you about it."

"Jack took the call?"

"No, I did, but I missed some others, mostly about speaking engagements and all that. He took them down."

Natalie turned her head. "Oh, come in, Timothy. Are we ready to start on the great project?"

"I am."

"What do we do first?"

"First," he drawled, sprawling in a big chair and laying a notebook on the table before him, "we make ourselves comfortable. Do you mind if I smoke?"

"Not at all." I saw her relax.

"Well, then," Tim began.

I gathered up the wastebasket of letters, took them into Tim's room and settled down at his big desk to sort them. He had an open portable on the desk and I moved it to one side to make more room, saw the paper, found myself reading:

Dear Hugh:

At first I thought you might be having a brainstorm, but I'll swear there's something in it. Clifford is working with a guy named Joe Bates, ostensibly here as a houseman though they are both notably shy about naming the employment agent.

My guess is that they have worked together before, that Bates sets up the victim and Clifford takes her.

Right now there is trouble between them, the well-known falling out of thieves. Bates wants quick action. Clifford wants time. It seems Mrs. C. changed her will recently, dividing her estate between C. and a niece she had never seen but for whose neglect she feels some sort of neurotic guilt. The niece is here now and it's my hunch C. wants to dispose of her, before further steps are taken with Natalie. Half a loaf, whatever they say, is not good enough.

I'm doing my best to run down some background on this Joe Bates. Natalie's maid, jealous as hell, believes C. tried twice to kill Natalie on their honeymoon. May be something in it, maybe not. No way of getting any proof. At any rate, the one I'm most worried about at this moment is the niece. She is obviously the number one target.

I could also bear to know the whereabouts of George Armstrong, big-time actor who went on the skids a few years ago and disappeared. Probably, like the flowers that bloom in the spring, he has nothing to do with the case.

I'll keep in touch.

I just made it to my own bathroom, where I was sick. When I had rinsed out my mouth and my head had stopped turning, I went back to sort the letters, trying to put them in chronological order, as some of them had been there for months. I kept the door open in case the telephone should ring, and twice ran down to answer it and take messages.

"At this rate," Jack commented from his place beside the drawing-room fire, where he was reading *The New York*

Times, "you're going to be worn to a shadow."

"Good for the figure," I assured him cheerfully.

There were steps on the porch and a metallic clatter.

"More mail," Jack said and went to bring it in from the box. There must have been thirty letters jammed together. "We'll have to get one of those big boxes they have on street corners if this goes on. You know, I'll never get used to Natalie being so famous. She's so modest about it that you'd never realize—except sometimes when she is thinking and you look at her you see her eyes and that sort of depth, as though they saw things we couldn't."

He shook his head. "You know, Constance, I used to try like mad to fight Alice's influence, because she wanted Natalie protected from the world, but damned if I'm not beginning to feel the same way." He waved a careless hand at the bundle of letters. "On your way, slave. Back to the salt mines."

I picked up the letters and went upstairs. They would go in the most recent pile, but first I automatically flipped through them. About halfway through there was an envelope addressed to Miss Constance Armstrong. I had not seen the handwriting for a long time, but I knew it was my father's. It had been mailed in New York.

Dearest Daughter:

A television program announced that Natalie and her husband have returned to Alcott and that you are a house guest there. For God's sake, get away. There must be some way I can help you. You can reach me care of General Delivery, New York City.

If you will accept it, I send you my love. That's hardly adequate, is it?

Your loving father.

Ten

I sorted the mail into separate piles, trying to keep it chronological. What I needed was a ball of twine to tie up the separate packets until I could answer them.

It was the first time I had gone to the kitchen, where I explained what I needed. Bates merely shook his head and made no attempt to help, but Freda produced what I wanted along with a pair of scissors.

I tied up the bundles and made a separate pile of business letters and bills that must be referred to Natalie. Then, because there was no other place for them, I tossed them back into the wastebasket and restored the typewriter to its former place. One thing sure, Tim would know damned well I had read that letter.

Letter! I felt in my sweater pocket for my father's letter, picked up and turned over the cushion on the chair, looked on the floor, and finally went through the bundles of letters, one by one. My father's letter was gone.

I tried to reconstruct my actions. Jack had given me the mail and I had not been downstairs since then except when I went to the kitchen to get the twine. I made one more search of Tim's room, searching again all the places I had searched before. Then I went downstairs, looking at each stair, my eyes on the floor as I went to the kitchen.

Freda was peeling potatoes and Bates was sitting on the edge of the kitchen table eating a doughnut. He got up belatedly as I came in, wiped his mouth, and tried to look ingratiating.

"If you want anything," Freda said rather sharply, and I knew my presence in the kitchen was unwelcome, "you only have to ring." I wondered what conference I had interrupted.

"I dropped a letter when I came down here for the twine," I said, my eyes traveling from the door to the cupboard where I had stood beside Freda.

Joe swallowed a bit of doughnut. "You didn't drop it here, Miss Armstrong."

"If you should find it—"

"Sure," he said. "Sure thing. Carrier pigeon service our specialty."

"Joe," his wife said warningly. "I'll take a good look, Miss Armstrong, but you didn't drop it here. I've just mopped the floor and I keep my counters spotless, if I do say so. Not a scrap of clutter around."

She looked calm enough but she was carefully whittling a potato down to the thickness of a lead pencil. She jabbed her finger with the paring knife and a drop of blood oozed out. She gave a little gasp and held her finger under the cold water tap to stop the bleeding. Bates ambled out of the room.

"Miss Armstrong," she said abruptly, "I guess you aren't planning to stay. You haven't put out your luggage to be stored. I don't blame you. This is no place for you." She added hastily, "With New York so near."

I went out. There was nothing else to do. But I knew they were lying. They had not only found but read that letter from my father, though why they should lie about it, what importance it could conceivably have for them, I could not make out. Nonetheless it made me uneasy, not only because it was the first intimation I had had that my father was alive, but because I felt instinctively that the

100

Bateses had no right to that letter.

As I reached the top of the stairs, Tim was coming out of the Cliffords' suite. He put a finger to his lips and ducked his head toward the door of his own room. In spite of his peremptory manner, I went in and he closed the door quietly.

I might as well get it over. "I read that letter in your typewriter," I said baldly.

"I meant you to. That's why I left it there. No one else is apt to come in the room after the maid gets through and I won't mail it from here. The name Hugh Evans might have an unpleasant association for someone." He broke off and pushed me gently into a big leather armchair, the kind that tilts back with a footrest. "What's happened to you?" he asked, his voice quiet but his eyes alert. "If it's about your father—about what I wrote—"

"It's about my father but not what you wrote about him or about me."

"I probably overstated," he said quickly. "I didn't mean you to be all shook up."

I managed a laugh of sorts at that. "Just a small hint of possible murder? Why should that upset a girl? No, it's more than that. This morning I got a letter from my father."

"What!"

At that explosive sound I instinctively shushed him. There is something catching about a conspiratorial atmosphere.

"May I see it?"

"I lost it."

"You—"

"Wait!" I told him about going down to the kitchen for twine to tie up the bundles of letters and how, afterwards, I could not find my father's letter. I described my search, and how I had gone down to the kitchen to inquire.

"It must have fallen out of my pocket and they're lying about it though I can't understand why. There was nothing —but Freda stood there trying to act cool and whittled a potato away to nothing and cut her finger and Joe bolted out of the room and then she said something about my going to New York."

"Do you remember what was in the letter?"

I recited it verbatim.

"No question in your mind that it was your father's writing?"

"I'm positive."

"No return address? No indication of where he is?"

"General Delivery, New York City."

Tim took his time lighting his pipe. "So he too seems to want you to leave this nest of vipers. It seems to be unanimous. Why don't you go, Kate? I've tried to lay it on the line for you. There's trouble brewing. Plenty of trouble. If you won't do it for your own sake, what about Natalie?"

"Well, what about Natalie?" I retorted. "If you are right, how long do you think she'd live if I were out of the way? They could convince her to cut me out of her will. So I've got to stay here. She's safe as long as I am around."

When he spoke, it was to offer no encouragement or display any admiration over my courage. "Do you hear voices too?"

"I'm not trying to be Joan of Arc or any other damned heroine," I said furiously, "but I just can't walk out and leave Natalie to her fate."

Tim heaved a deep sigh, got up to knock out his pipe and then he deliberately took me in his arms. He kissed me on each cheek. "If you're so hell-bent on getting a medal, there's one for you," he said in a loverlike tone and I found myself laughing, though I was still shaking. "I can do a lot better than that," he assured me, "but this is not the time nor is it the place. And speaking of places, you'd better get out of my room before someone has ideas about dalliance and so forth and so forth."

"No further advice from the expert crime solver?" I tried to speak lightly, dismissing the kisses as of no account, which seemed to amuse him.

"Yes," he said abruptly. "Write to your father at General Delivery and I'll mail your letter today. Tell him someone found his letter and ask him not to go to General Delivery again, as someone might be looking for him. And tell him when he writes again, as you hope he will, to use a type-writer."

"You think someone wants to hurt my father?"

"I hve a weird idea that someone has already hurt your father. What Bates knows Clifford will know. But the chief point is this: he's your vulnerable point. It doesn't take long for anyone to get a taste of your quality, darling. Here you are all ready to run interference and protect Natalie, whom you barely know. What are you prepared to do for your father? And if it becomes a choice between the two—"

He slid an arm around me, not amorously but because he was aware my knees were shaking. "You get into your own room and write to your father. I'll take the letter to the post office this afternoon." He gave me a light spank across the hips. "Run along now. And try, when you come down for lunch, not to look suspicious or frightened or anything but your usual self. You haven't much of a poker face, you know."

"I'll try," I said with unexpected meekness, and I went in to write my letter. It was a harder task than I had ex-pected, because I didn't want to alarm my father but I wanted to warn him. So I told him not to expect any more mail from the GPO or to go near the place, and how to disguise any further letter of his.

"Only please, please write again. Your letter made me happier than I've been since Mother died. I miss you terribly. Don't keep away from me, Father. Please don't. We'll work things out together. I don't know who stole your letter or why, and it may mean nothing, but just remember that I have two good friends here: Natalie and Timothy Struthers, the writer who is to work on her biography and who is really here to try to find out what is wrong. I love you very much. Constance."

II

It was as an act of defiance that I stacked my luggage outside the door for Bates to put in the storeroom, my declaration of intention to stay indefinitely in Alcott. Natalie, leaving her room early for the cocktail hour, saw my open door and hearing the radio, came to smile and wave at me.

"What a nice idea! I should have thought of that myself."

"You've thought of everything else," I told her. "Even having the spinet tuned."

"Someday I want to hear you play."

"You'd run screaming for help after five minutes. So far I'm just fumbling around. No technique. Nothing. With difficulty I might be able to hammer out 'Three Blind Mice.'"

"Well, don't sacrifice too much time on those tiresome letters. Spend as much as you like practicing."

"You're really a darling, Natalie!"

"This seems like a ghost house. Where is everyone?"

"Tim has gone to the post office, Bates is doing some shopping for Freda, and Jack is down in the basement where, he tells me, he is fixing up a workshop."

"Oh, dear God," Natalie wailed in amused dismay. "Why that man thinks he can repair anything— Don't tell me! There will be bolts and screws all over the place and they will never, never get together again."

"He can't do much harm now," I consoled her. "He promised to sharpen the knives which Freda says are too dull to cut butter."

"Oh," Natalie said flatly. She stared at me, the great sunken eyes almost blind, and then she groped in the pocket of the lime wool dress and I saw the glimmer of a silver chain as she reached for her lucky piece. I had forgotten about her obsession with knives and wished heartily I could learn to guard my tongue.

Aware that I was staring at her, she summoned up a smile. "I'm so glad you've decided to stay," she said, indicating the suitcases stacked outside my door. "Are they labeled? Oh, good, because the storeroom is huge but a complete mess. Everything seems to end there sooner or later, and as this house has been lived in by one family for a hundred and fifty years, you may have some idea of the state of confusion."

"My mother made a recording of her Town Hall debut which she left behind. Is there any chance it still exists, that it could be here? I'd dearly love to listen to it."

"It's probably somewhere in the general chaos. Someday we'll go up and see whether we can unearth it."

She went down the stairs. From the back she looked like a girl, she was so slim and erect and her walk was youthful, nor was there a single strand of white in that soft dusky black cloud of hair.

The radio was playing a Mozart quintet almost too low to hear. As I reached for the volume knob, I heard someone dialing, heard Natalie say, her voice almost a whisper, "Mr. Grace?" I turned up the knob hastily, shutting off her voice. This time I was not going to eavesdrop but I couldn't help wondering why Natalie should have answered this call rather than any of the others and why she had been so anxious to make sure that everyone was out of the way while she did so.

After we had gathered in the drawing room for cocktails, Jack came running up from the basement. Tim, as he passed me, made a faint signal with thumb and forefinger to indicate that the letter had been mailed.

"There's sawdust in your hair," Natalie said.

"Sorry, love. I started fixing up that spare room in the basement where the family used to store the winter coal and I got carried away. I'm going to build some shelves and I'm making a list of tools I'll need as well as a really solid workbench and a place for some power tools."

"You sound very professional," Tim commented.

"Oh, it's just play, but it's absorbing. I thought I'd arrange for someplace to keep stuff for winter emergencies: candles, kerosene, fuses, maybe some Presto logs if the furnace goes off, enough to see us through a North Pole winter." Jack laughed at his own enthusiasm. "How did the first session go?"

"What do you think, Timothy?" Natalie asked. "So far as I could see, we just rode off in all directions."

"That's the general idea. I used to try to make people stick to what I thought was important, but I discovered that what was important to me was not important to them. I learned in time that when the name of Uncle Jim kept recurring it was because Uncle Jim was a major part of the story and had some real significance if I could find it."

"I thought your approach would be different. That you'd ask, When were you born? What do you remember about your parents and your early childhood? That sort of thing."

"You can't tap memory like that. An old tune, a flavor, a scent—well, Proust illustrated that once and for all. The thing is that memory is tricky. Whip it and it balks. Let it alone and it works for you."

"Sounds fascinating," Jack commented. Then he gave his engaging grin. "But actually I don't know a thing about it. You're both way ahead of me." He broke off as he saw Bates hovering beside his chair. "Yes?"

"My wife wants to know what you did with that carving knife. All you brought up were the paring knives."

Jack grinned ruefully. "Sorry, I made a hash of that. Took the edge right off, didn't know my own strength, so I guess it's beyond saving. I'll pick up another in the village tomorrow."

Natalie spilled her sherry and wiped up the wet spot on her dress with her cocktail napkin.

"I'll pour you another," Jack said.

"Not now."

"Do you good. You're getting nervous. What you need is exercise."

She groaned. "But, Jack, this isn't Sicily. It's Connecticut. It's practically November."

"Tomorrow we walk. That's an order. We won't go far, a nice gentle stroll, bundled up warm, and you can smell the autumn leaves. Someone is breaking the law by building bonfires, but they smell wonderful and tangy. A few more weeks and there will be pumpkins on the ground."

"We-ll," she smiled reluctantly. "Tomorrow then. But not too far. And no church towers."

He gave a shout of laughter. "No church towers. But once you got over being lame after that exercise, you ate so much you put on three pounds in a week."

"Kill or cure," Natalie said. "That's my husband's method." She added, and her voice was flat, "Kill or cure."

Eleven

Natalie went to bed early that night, saying with a laughing glance at her husband that she had to prepare for the next day's exercise. She was halfway up the stairs when the telephone rang. As usual I took the message, this one from the local librarian asking whether Miss Netherfield would give a reading of her poems some afternoon in the near future. They would serve lemonade and iced cakes and make a real party of it and such a privilege for the people of Alcott who were so proud of their famous poet.

When I came back, Tim was laughing. "You sound as though you had been at the White House switchboard for a year. Assured, polite, but firm."

"You have to be firm with these people. Otherwise they'd be storming the house."

Natalie gave a gasp of dismay.

"You might put up a simple warning on the door," Tim suggested.

"For instance?" Jack asked.

"Smallpox."

Jack grinned and then sobered. "After all, we're living in the house of a famous woman. Imagine how people in a hundred years will envy the ones who had that privilege. They will wonder what she was really like. Was she as beautiful as her photographs? Was she a bacchante like Millay or a mystic like Dickinson, or retreating from life like Browning or—well, what can anyone say about Sappho?"

"Dear God!" Natalie exclaimed, amused.

"On the whole I think the neighbors have been very reasonable," Jack said. "Naturally they want to see Natalie. Someday there will be a plaque on the house reading: NATALIE NETHERFIELD LIVED HERE, and people will come to see it. A pilgrimage."

"My dear!" Natalie expostulated.

"I mean it."

She blew him a kiss and I saw his expression when he looked at her, poised, slim, graceful and young on the staircase. Romeo looking up at Juliet on the balcony.

"Oh, Constance," she said, "if Mr. Grace should call me again, let me know, will you? At any time. Even if I am resting. He is the only person who can provide the real historical background of the Netherfields. He did a book on Alcott once that contains a lot of material on the family. Unfortunately the book is out of print and he can't get hold of his own copy, somewhere in his house in Florida, which is closed when he is away. But he can give me material I can't get anywhere else."

"Why not ask him up here for a visit?" Jack suggested. "He sounds like a bonanza for Struthers."

"Unfortunately he comes to New York for just a few days at a time and he is always rushed off his feet with appointments."

"How about a movie?" Tim asked me. I had already noticed that there was no television in the house. Natalie could not watch the screen because it gave her blinding headaches. Usually Jack read bits from the newspaper to her, but she did not attempt to read them herself. I knew now why her eyes had that wide look which was so fascinating. She could not bear to conceal them behind glasses, which she must have found worthwhile because she paid a heavy price in headaches. During my preliminary look at the letters in her room she had rather sheepishly pulled a small magnifying glass out of her pocket to verify a name.

"Come on," Tim insisted. "Let's taste the dissipations of Alcott, drink life to the dregs."

Jack laughed. "One movie, one drugstore fountain and, if you are really adventurous, a hamburger stand much patronized by truck drivers, where there is a very loud jukebox."

I went up to get my coat. Alice's voice could be heard even from behind Natalie's closed door, scolding her for agreeing to go for a walk the next day. She would catch cold; she would get a sore throat; she might have pneumonia and she hadn't had a flu shot this year.

When I came out of my room, wearing my coat and carrying a wool scarf, Freda was coming down the attic stairs, which ran up beside my room. There were two doors at the top, one leading to the servants' rooms and the other to the big storage space Natalie had described.

"I've been putting away your suitcases because the stairs aren't good for Joe. He has a bad heart and he's overweight, but I can't get him to watch his diet."

"Sorry to make you that extra trouble."

Freda looked at me. "So you are going to stay, after all."

"For a while, at least."

She went past my door, stopped, turned back. "I guess we all think we know our own business best."

"It's a lovely house."

"Yeah, but I wish to God I was out of it and that's a fact."

"Then why do you stay?"

She shrugged. "I go where Joe goes and don't ask me why." There was a puzzled expression on her face. "He's not good-looking, he's not easy to get along with, he always has to have his own way, he won't listen to reason." She almost wailed. "He never listens!" Then she pulled herself

110

together. "I guess I'm the restless type. I'm not used to country living." She trudged down the stairs.

Tim caught up with me as I reached the first floor. "Got a pencil that needs sharpening?" he asked in a low tone.

I shook my head, puzzled.

"Well, all in the interests of science—or something." He pulled a penknife out of his pocket, opened the front door a crack, put the blade into the crack and bent it until it snapped off.

"What on earth—?"

"I'm going down to see whether this can be soldered in place in the famous workshop. Won't take a minute."

It was nearer ten minutes before he came back, took my arm and ushered me out of the house, closing the door quietly behind him. "Do you mind walking? It's only about six blocks. If I get out the car now, they'll wonder what I've been doing all this time."

"What have you been doing?"

"Always the direct approach," Tim said. "To tell you the truth—"

"Aha!"

"No skepticism from you, woman. I have been eavesdropping."

"That's becoming quite a habit, isn't it?" I laughed up at him, but there was no response.

"Look, Kate, you've simply got to get the hell out of here and do it at once. I'd like to drive you to New York tomorrow, but that would cause a lot of comment we could do without. Suppose you telephone Mr. Fowler from the drugstore or wherever there's a pay phone and ask him to call you in the morning, saying he has a perfect job for you but it must be filled at once."

"And how can I explain that?"

"You won't need to explain it. As I told you before, he will be delighted to get you out of here."

"For fear I'll try to lure Jack away from his wife?"

"Whatever the reason. What the hell does it matter? Just get away."

"And leave Natalie to her fate, I suppose."

"I'm not concerned with Natalie."

"I am. And you aren't the first to try to uproot me. Mr. Fowler wants me out, my father wants me out, Alice wants me out, Freda gave me another warning tonight. But I'm staying, Tim, until Natalie is safe."

We were walking at a fast clip because of the biting wind that stung my cheeks and made me gasp for breath. I pulled the wool scarf over my head and wrapped it around my neck.

"When I went down to the basement workroom, our friend Bates was issuing an ultimatum. He said he'd had it. Working his fingers to the bone, a touch I rather fancied, as he never lifts a finger if he can avoid it. Anyhow he said no more putting off, no more excuses, no more attempting to change plans. And we're not, he said, going to cut our losses. When Clifford asked what he meant, he said, 'You know damned well. You're willing to stand by and let the girl get half. I say the hell with that. We work and we work fast. The girl first. Then the dame. It's now or never.' "

Tim's hand tightened on my arm. "You all right?"

"It's like an old melodrama, isn't it, or some Grade B gangster film. I can't believe it."

"You'd better believe it."

"And Jack—just—gave in?"

"No, he seems to be having qualms, whether about you or his easy life or the risk or whatever, I wouldn't know. Anyhow, he said if Bates made a move he'd call the police about him. And Bates said, 'You mean about us. We rise or sink together, pal.' "

On that cheery note we reached the movie theater. There was nowhere else to go out of the cold and we sat there for

112

a couple of hours. If we looked at the screen, I have no idea of what we saw. What I was chiefly aware of was Tim's hand holding mine. It was a nice feeling and comforting. About the only comfort that night afforded.

We stopped at the drugstore for hot chocolate and Tim made a call to his friend Hugh Evans. He didn't explain to me beyond saying he was calling out the reserves. "I want Bates watched all the time and I mean all the time."

We went back to the house at a fast clip, the wind fairly pushing us along. The house was quiet when Tim let us in with the key Jack had given him.

"Don't leave any incriminating letters or notes around your room," he whispered, his lips almost against my ear. "This afternoon I got a lock for my briefcase, just in case. And you lock your door, don't you?"

"Of course not. It would seem awfully queer to lock myself in, in a private house."

"Lock it." When I made no reply, he said urgently, "Promise me."

I nodded, turning toward him, and somehow his lips brushed my cheek and found my mouth. It was a moment of unexpected sweetness. Then he released me, whispered, "Good night, darling," and I went up to my room. After a moment, I locked the door as quietly as I could.

II

The following morning passed as the others had done. Bates served breakfast in his usual surly manner, wheezing with every step. I noticed there was no exchange of greetings between him and Jack, though the latter seemed to be keeping a close eye on him.

Tim went up to work with Natalie, and Jack, with a laughing apology for his failure of the day before, went out to replace the carving knife he had ruined.

113

I spent the morning in Tim's room, typing brief acknowledgments to some of Natalie's letters, explaining the long delay resulting in a lack of forwarding address and Natalie's temporary fatigue.

At lunchtime both Natalie and Tim were in high spirits, so apparently the session had gone well. Jack reported his progress in building shelves, confessing that somehow there seemed to be a lot of shavings around, but he'd ask Bates to clear up the mess. Bates, serving a casserole of escalloped potatoes, nearly dropped it in my lap when he heard that, but he made no comment.

I watched for the mail, but there was no letter from my father. Of course he could not have received mine until this morning. There were fewer local calls now, but the special article in the *Times* had brought an increase in mail. I could hear the rattle of Tim's typewriter and closed my door and settled down at the spinet for an hour of slow, careful practice, listening to every note, the concentration preventing me from listening to all the warning voices in my ear.

I was startled when my door was flung open and Natalie almost fell into the room. She closed the door and sagged against it, her face colorless, her breath shallow and quick.

"Natalie!" I helped her into the rocking chair and knelt beside her, watching anxiously. At last her eyes lost their blind look and she put in my hand a piece of paper on which words had been written in red chalk which had smeared, making them hard to decipher:

> You are in danger. Don't trust anyone. Watch yourself. I see a knife threatening you.

"Where did you find this?" I asked.
"It was lying on the floor in my sitting room."
"Where's the envelope?"
She shook her head.

"No envelope? Then it's someone in the house."

"Someone in the house," she said, her voice colorless.

"Have you shown this to Jack?"

"No!"

"But—"

The hand that gripped mine convulsively was feverish.

"I'm sure," I said as calmly as I could, "this is someone's idea of a joke. You can't ignore it, in any case. The police—"

"No."

"Then," I said, "I'll write to Mr. Fowler."

After a long time she nodded her head, sipped the glass of water I gave her, and went back to her room.

I wrote a hasty letter to Mr. Fowler, enclosing the red-chalk note, and describing Natalie's reactions. "She won't tell Jack or notify the police. But perhaps you will know what should be done. I don't honestly feel that her judgment should be trusted, because she is too overwrought." Then I went out to drop the letter in the box for the mailman.

Tim was still busy at his typewriter and anyhow I had no authorization from Natalie to confide in him. It occurred to me that this would be a good time to go up to the attic and see whether I could find the recording of my mother's Town Hall debut. The storage room was enormous, but the rafters were unexpectedly low and some of them were so broad they too had been used for storage purposes.

I looked around in dismay at the discards of a hundred and fifty years—harmoniums, old rockers, broken tables, shattered lamps, worn rugs wrapped in burlap. Nothing had been thrown away. There were trunks, so many of them that my heart sank, but they were neatly labeled with their contents, which saved hours of time and back-breaking labor. Even with all this secondhand store atmosphere, the windowpanes were clean and there were no cobwebs. At least I need not be afraid of bats and spiders and other horrors that lurk in neglected attics.

There was a wooden box with a printed label: "Florence's belongings, misc." It had been nailed shut and I struggled until I forced one board loose and then managed to open it. There was a smell of mothballs, a lovely sable coat, and under that, tossed in carelessly, an ivory comb and brush set, a Venetian glass perfume bottle, dresses thrown in anyhow, and underneath, a record case, reading *Town Hall Debut.*

I slid the record out of its case and held it up to the light. It had not been broken, but a sharp knife had been driven over and over it, defacing it completely. I put back gently the clothes that had been thrown into Florence's box. She had left without taking clothes, or toilet articles, or even that magnificent sable. And, seeing how her belongings had been treated, the vicious defacing of her record, I thought that her elopement must, in part, have been a kind of flight. She had gone, driven not only by love but by fear.

I tried to console myself, crouching over that pathetic box; she had had those years of great happiness and shared love, the days when my father's reputation and popularity were at their peak, when we could go nowhere without people staring, thronging about my father for autographs, envying my mother. They had, of course, gone to the usual first nights and to some of the Hollywood parties, but not to the big noisy ones.

Our own house, as I remember it, had been simple but large enough to accommodate a secretary to handle my father's stacks of fan mail and his business contracts, and a Mexican couple who adored them both, and, until I reached school age, a nurse for me.

I could remember my surprise at school at being pointed out as George Armstrong's daughter, at being treated as something special, because none of the movie atmosphere ever entered the house.

In the evenings, when my parents did not entertain, and they did so rarely and most informally, my mother would play the piano or they would play backgammon and gin rummy and occasionally chess, or discuss his newest role and how it should be played.

The change had come so gradually that I had not been aware of it until Father was definitely going downhill, having difficulty in getting parts. Neither my father nor my mother wanted me to be worried about what they both believed, for a long time, to be merely a run of bad luck. Whatever gossip circulated, I was never permitted to hear it. And then the world fell apart, the house was sold, Father even did extras and walk-ons, and then, when Mother got a job clerking in a dress shop, he wrote his pathetic letter and went away, out of our lives.

How long I crouched beside that box, I don't know. A loose paper on the floor rose, fluttered and dropped again and I supposed someone had opened the door to the attic stairs, causing a draft.

I brushed my cheeks with the backs of my hands, wiping away the silly tears. Looking back served no purpose. The condition of the box made it clear that someone had wanted to destroy every vestige of Florence. Someone had hated her. And now someone wanted to destroy Natalie. But first someone had to eliminate me if he was to have the whole loaf. I didn't know how much capital one must have to draw fifty thousand a year in income, but it must be a lot.

A stair creaked and I got swiftly to my feet, too swiftly, because I hit my head a great crack against one of the low rafters. I don't even remember striking the floor.

Twelve

The first thing I was aware of was a brilliant flash of light, followed by a tremendous crash. The ceiling light flickered and went out. I was lying on the attic floor in the dark. I was cold and I had the most godawful headache I had ever experienced. It pounded, it sent lancing pains through my eyes. I couldn't see anything. I couldn't hear. Then there was another brilliant jagged flash through the windowpane and the heavy rumbling came again. An electric storm. I knew that much. And the power was off again.

I tried to get up, but I couldn't manage it. Every motion made my head hurt unbearably and my legs refused to bear me. I put my hand up to my head and my fingers were sticky with warm blood. I needed help, but the house was so well-built I couldn't make anyone hear me. My cheek was wet with blood, so I knew I'd have to have help. I wasn't specially worried because I knew scalp wounds bled a lot, but I was so weak I was afraid that if I didn't move soon I wouldn't be able to move at all. I might not be found for hours. Or, like the bride who hid in the chest—oh, shut up, I told myself crossly, things are bad enough without creating imaginary horrors.

There was a tremendous flash and a crack of thunder that came almost simultaneously. It seemed as though the house itself must have been struck.

I heard Tim shout, "Where's Kate?"

There was a jumble of voices, so I knew the attic door must be open and then Tim shouted again, "Damn it, she couldn't be out in this storm. We've got to find her."

"But what," Jack demanded, "do you think could have happened to her?"

"Your guess is as good as mine," Tim snapped. "Probably better."

"Just what do you mean by that?"

"Cut the talking and let's get to work. Find her. Find her now."

"You're right," Jack said, and I could hear the alarm in his voice. "Bates! Bates!"

"Yeah?" came the wheeze.

"Have you seen Miss Armstrong?"

"Not since lunch."

"Get candles and that lantern we found in the basement and some flashlights. Anything. I'll take the attic. Freda, you go through every room. Struthers—"

"I'll take the basement."

I cried out but there was only a whimper. I tried to move, but I had twisted my leg under me and my knee hurt like blazes. Perhaps if I could crawl, dragging the painful leg—

I tried to yell in answer to the cries echoing through the house of "Constance! Kate! Miss Armstrong!"

The telephone rang and, to my astonishment, I heard Natalie call, "I'll answer it," Natalie with her terror of storms not only venturing from her room but going down to the phone.

I saw a gleam of light and feet pounded up the attic stairs. There was a dim figure behind the lantern, which moved slowly from side to side.

"Constance!" Jack called, but he was holding the lantern too high; it was at the level of the trunks and I was on the floor. He turned to go back and I managed a desperate sort of whimper. He whirled around, the lantern found me. I

119

must have been a horrifying sight; my face, as I saw later, covered with blood, blood on my clothes, blood on my hands, my left leg twisted at an unlikely angle.

Jack let out a shout. "She's up here. I think she's hurt. Get a doctor right away!"

It was typical of Bates to wheeze, "I don't know any names to call."

"Get out the car and go to the hospital or call an ambulance."

"In this storm?"

"Ask Mrs. Clifford who her doctor is. Now, on your way, Bates. That's an order."

Jack bent over, picking me up gently, muttering, "Oh, my God! Oh, my God!" He hung the lantern over one wrist to guide him and started slowly, carefully, down the steep attic stairs. At the foot of the stairs Tim was waiting with the Bateses.

Freda cried out, "What happened to her?"

"I think she knocked herself out on one of those low beams. I nearly did it myself when I took up my luggage," Jack said.

"She's covered with blood."

"Just a scalp wound, I think, but there's something wrong with her left leg. Bates, if you don't get started in one minute, I'll break your neck."

"What happened? What happened? How do you feel?" The barrage of questions fell on my ears. I tried to answer, tried to keep my eyes open, but it was too much trouble.

"I'll take her," Tim said.

"She's all right," Jack answered. "She hasn't fainted. She's just resting. You take this lantern."

My head was against Jack's broad chest and I felt as safe as though I were in my own bed. I turned my head slightly, settling more firmly in the strong grasp of his arms.

It was Freda who got me to bed. Only when I was in my

120

own room did Alice put in an appearance and wash off the blood that stained my face and hands and neck while Freda undressed me, being unexpectedly gentle and jarring my head as little as possible. She did not attempt to straighten out my left leg though she did touch it carefully.

"I think it may be dislocated, Miss Armstrong. I'm pretty sure it isn't broken."

I had my eyes open now and I saw that Alice was looking strained and Freda was ghastly, her skin was almost gray.

As there was another flash and crash of thunder that came almost simultaneously, I found myself speaking aloud for the first time. "Poor Natalie!"

"I've got her in her own room," Alice said, "and if she gets any more upset I'll give her one of those painkillers." Her smile was almost sly. "When her husband made her give them up, I put some aside. I guess I know Miss Natalie better than he does. What with her headaches and a storm like this, I won't answer for her without one of the pills. And on top of everything else, just when I'm worried about her and she needs me, Miss Armstrong gets herself hurt and sets Miss Natalie into a great fuss when she should be keeping quiet."

"I'll stay with Miss Armstrong," Freda said.

"Well, I'm glad to have that off my mind. What with Mr. Clifford looking after Miss Armstrong, carrying her around practically snuggled up in his arms—" She flung out of the room, muttering.

Freda set the lantern on the dressing table and drew up the rocking chair beside the bed. Once she put her hand on my forehead, once she took my pulse. As I looked at her questioningly, she smiled. "I trained as a nurse but I found I was more interested in cooking food than in what happened to it once people ate it."

I found myself laughing feebly, which hurt my head.

"You haven't a fever. Shock and a gash in your scalp,

probably a slight concussion, and a dislocated knee. It must hurt dreadfully, but all you can do now is to lie quietly until the doctor comes."

She sat staring at nothing, her face drawn and colorless. I turned my head as easily as I could and looked around the room. While I had been in the attic, someone had done a thorough job of ransacking my bureau drawers.

"Those rafters," Freda said at last. "They ought at least to be whitewashed so people could see them. There was no way of telling how you had hit yourself." She was watching my face carefully, so it was simpler to close my eyes and pretend to doze. The ransacking of my room, the creak on the stairs, the draft I had felt from the open door, all added up to more than an accidental blow against a low rafter.

But sleep was impossible. Jack was knocking at Natalie's door, demanding to be admitted, and Alice was refusing. Mrs. Clifford was trying to sleep and she was not to be disturbed.

"That's nonsense. Storms send her almost out of her mind. She needs me. Let me in, woman, or I'll break this door down and you'll be out on your neck tomorrow. Is that clear?"

The door opened. I heard Jack exclaim, "Darling, why didn't you send for me? You know I've helped you through these things before."

"Not now, dear. I found one of those old painkillers and I'm half asleep. Just let me rest. I won't try to go down to dinner. And would you mind if Alice makes up the bed in your room?"

"Of course not. Sure you'll be all right?"

"Quite sure."

Again there was a jagged flash of lightning, but this time more seconds passed before I heard the thunder. The storm must be moving away.

For once Bates had been efficient. He arrived sooner than anyone would have expected, with the doctor. And at that moment the lights came on, the oil burner began to hum and the house was alive again.

At Jack's instructions, Bates took the doctor's dripping raincoat and there was a jumble of voices as Jack and Tim tried to explain what had happened.

"Oh," the doctor exclaimed, "I thought it was Mrs. Clifford. I've seen her through the nerve crises that attend bad storms before."

"See Miss Armstrong has every care, Doctor," Jack said. "That this should happen to her in my wife—in our house!"

"All right, all right. Suppose you let me see the patient."

He came up the stairs and Freda, with her nurse's training, was on her feet instantly. "I can help, Doctor. I trained at Massachusetts General."

The doctor was tall and slim and casual in manner but not casual in his examination, though he was as careful as possible not to hurt me. He went over my head with gentle fingers, watching my face when I winced, and once as he touched a painful spot I gave a muffled cry.

He smiled at me. "Slight concussion and a break in the skin. What hit you?"

Freda's stubby fingers gripped together; her eyes never left my face.

"I don't remember exactly. I think I stood up and cracked my head against one of those low rafters."

"Well, there's not too much harm done." He grinned when he saw my expression. "Oh, you've got the granddaddy of all headaches, but I can fix that for you. There may be a little fever before morning. I'll have the drugstore send along some stuff, but someone ought to sit up with you tonight."

"I can do that," Freda said. "Let Alice get dinner for once in her life. And I can take over for the night without any difficulty."

"I'm most grateful to you," the doctor said. "I'm sure we all are. Now let's take a look at that leg."

This time I let out a yell after he had prodded and pressed and abruptly gave a hard jerk.

"Sorry," he said. "It was dislocated and that was the quickest way to get it back into place. I know it hurts like hell, but in the long run you won't have any trouble. Keep off it for a day or so and then use a cane until it can bear your weight without hurting you. Maybe a little massage would help—but not tonight."

As I moaned he said, "I'll send up some painkiller. Oh, Mrs. Clifford may have some. Powerful stuff she uses now and then for those severe headaches of hers. We'll see if we can borrow some."

He went out of the room and came back shortly, carrying a bottle. He unscrewed the top and pulled out the cotton. "Good. This is a new bottle. She says she hasn't been using the stuff recently. I thought she looked like a different woman, except for the inevitable results of the electric storm. Queer the things that can terrorize the most intelligent people."

He turned to Freda. "One of these now. One in four hours. If she is in a lot of pain, you can give her a third in another four hours. But that's it. No more." He hesitated and then shook out three pills and pocketed the bottle. "I'll return this to Mrs. Clifford. Even if things seem bad," he told me, "you'll make it and be right as rain in a few days. You're a healthy young woman. You'll probably sleep for hours." He grinned at me. "I hope." He plunged the needle of a hypodermic into my arm.

"As you've had your training," he told Freda, "you'll know if any real complication develops. In that case, of course, you can call me. I'm the last surviving medical man who pays house calls. You'll know whether it is necessary. You can expect a bit of fever later on."

"I can handle it," Freda said competently. She went into my bathroom and came back with a glass of water and gave me one of the pills. The other two she put in an envelope on my dressing table and out of my reach. The doctor nodded approvingly. He gave me a pat on the shoulder and said, "I'll just take a look at Mrs. Clifford before I go."

Freda glanced at her watch. "I'll have to arrange things so Alice will know what to do about dinner. I'll tell her to stay with you until I can take over."

"I'll be all right when I stop hurting so much," I said. "I won't need anyone with me."

For a moment Freda stood looking at me anxiously, reluctant to leave me alone. Then with a little half-despairing gesture, she went out. "I'll leave your door open in case you want anything. Call if you do. Call real loud."

But she didn't go downstairs. She went quietly up the uncarpeted stairs to the attic. I did not hear her come down. The shot had begun to take effect and the pain in my knee and my head subsided.

Natalie's door must be open too, because I heard the doctor say, "You needn't worry about your niece. The damage is only temporary though it's painful, of course. The resemblance startled me. The girl is so much like you anyone would take her for your daughter."

"I know," Natalie said.

"Mrs. Bates tells me she's a trained nurse and she has offered to sit up with my patient tonight if your maid can manage with the dinner."

"Of course. Personally I don't want any dinner. I'm going to rest and I don't want to be disturbed."

The doctor said a cheery "good night" and then I heard Freda coming down the attic stairs. She stopped abruptly

125

when she saw Jack standing in the hall outside my room.

"Looking for something?" Jack asked rather sharply.

"I was wondering—"

"Well?" I had never heard that tone in his pleasant voice before.

"There are no bloodstains on any of the low rafters," Freda said. "I guess Miss Armstrong doesn't know what hit her." She went past him and down the stairs.

Jack came into my room. "How do you feel?"

"Like hell warmed over."

He came closer to the bed. "How did you manage to give yourself such a crack?"

I let my eyes close drowsily. "I can't remember. It's just a blank."

"Well—oh, what's that, Alice?"

"I'll take over now. No call for you to be in Miss Armstrong's room."

He went out without a word and I opened my eyes cautiously. Alice settled herself with a flounce in the rocking chair. "You'd think there was trouble enough without this. Poor Miss Natalie scared of the storm and now she has one of those headaches she gets when she's upset. And a lot you care."

"I have a headache too."

"Serves you right. Trying to vamp Mr. Clifford practically in front of his wife's nose. Lying there in his arms with your head on his shoulder. Trouble is Mrs. Clifford is too trusting. You and your mother—troublemakers, both of you."

From downstairs I heard Jack call, "Bates, where are you? Well, get up here, I want to talk to you."

"No need to yell with Mrs. Clifford trying to sleep," Alice said. "I'll put a flea in his ear." She bounced out of the room while the chair rocked wildly over a squeaking board.

126

"Pst!"

I turned my head painfully and grunted with the lancing pain. Tim had stuck his head inside the door. "What really happened?" he whispered.

"I'm supposed to have knocked myself out on a low rafter."

"Are you sure?"

"No, I'm not sure. Freda looked and says there's no blood on any of the rafters."

"Freda said so?"

"The worst of it is that I'm stuck here. If a letter comes from my father—"

"I'll check the mail when it comes in the morning until you feel a lot better. And why the hell is your door open? I told you to lock it."

"How can I?" I asked reasonably. "Anyhow, Freda is going to sit up with me all night."

"The hell she is!" Tim frowned.

"She's a trained nurse."

"Okay. I'll keep my door open and check on you every half hour."

"That's absurd." I yawned, closed my eyes.

"Helpless as a baby," Tim muttered. He tiptoed to the bed, kissed me lightly on the chin, and went out, leaving the door open.

I must have slept heavily for a long time. When I awakened, the storm was over and the night was quiet. Freda saw that I was awake and came to touch my forehead lightly and to take my pulse.

"How do you feel?"

I found it too difficult to speak, but I managed to smile reassuringly at her before I went back to sleep.

The next time I awakened it was because my leg was hurting so badly that whenever I moved, the pain throbbed from ankle to hip. I moaned and tried to stifle the sound.

127

Freda was beside me in a moment, moving with the quiet precision of a nurse. "What is it?" She spoke just above a whisper.

"My leg. When I move."

She glanced at her watch. "You can have one of those painkillers." She went into the bathroom to fill a glass with water and Tim appeared in the doorway, wearing a heavy sweater and thick slacks, his hair tousled.

"Okay?"

"My leg hurts. I'm going to have a painkiller. For heaven's sake, what time is it?"

"Just about three. Low time of the night."

"Haven't you slept at all?"

"I'll make up tomorrow. Anyhow I can take a lot more than the loss of a night's sleep and not go into a decline."

"But I'm all right," I assured him.

"You'd better be." He turned to see Freda in the bathroom door, looking from one of us to the other. She pulled herself together with an effort.

"She's all right, Mr. Struthers. Just pain in her leg, which is to be expected. But there's no fever and she's been sleeping like a baby all night."

"A drugged baby."

"Doctor's orders and better than the pain." As Tim lingered uncertainly, she said, "She'll be all right, Mr. Struthers. I promise you." Which was an odd way of putting it.

Thirteen

Next morning a sullen Alice brought my breakfast tray. A weary Freda piled pillows behind me, brought me a damp cloth to wash my face and hands, and went off to get some sleep.

The toast was burned, the half grapefruit had not been cut, the egg was puffy as though it had been fried in some heavy cooking oil, the coffee had spilled onto the saucer.

Alice slammed the tray down with a kind of defiance. She did not ask how I felt, which was just as well. I felt awful. My mouth was like cotton wool, my head throbbed, my eyes hurt when I turned them from side to side, and my knee was so painful I was afraid to move it. Although the doctor had instructed me to stay off it, I didn't want any of Alice's ministrations I could avoid, so I asked her to help me into the bathroom.

"I guess I can do that," she said ungraciously. "Mrs. Clifford said not to disturb her until she rings. Those headaches of hers are horrible things, and I thought she'd got over them." Alice glared at me as though I were responsible. "I suppose I can help you, though you'd be better off at the hospital where they are prepared to look after people like you. And everything falling on me at once." Her anger seemed out of all proportion to the situation. "Freda has to catch up on sleep, leaving me to do the cooking, which I never liked and wasn't paid for. And Bates looks as though he'd been in a brawl. I always suspected he was a drinking man. Black eye coming up something wonderful, and his nose swollen twice its size, and bruises like he'd been losing in a prizefight. So he's laid up too, though he's not fit to be seen around, in any case. And Mr. Clifford is as haggard as though he hadn't slept for a week. Worry about his wife. She'd been so fine until just now." And Alice looked at me with angry, accusing eyes. I wondered if the woman was quite normal where Natalie was concerned.

The trip to the bathroom was something to forget as soon as possible but, by putting my weight on my right foot, I managed finally to clean my teeth, my head throbbing with every move, brushed my hair into some semblance of order, as well as I could, handicapped by the bandage the doctor had applied to the gash on my scalp. Alice got out a pair of fresh pajamas, but my leg wasn't flexible enough and she substituted a nightgown, which I could slip over my head, and I put on the taffeta dressing gown. When she had made up the bed, muttering as though she had to scrub an acre of floor on her knees, I got back onto it, with pillows behind me and the patchwork quilt over me.

It must have taken half an hour for the pain to subside to the point where I could think of anything but my body. People who praise illness as bringing out the best in people ought to have their heads examined. Pain forces you to think about yourself, directs your interest to your own body and what is happening to it. You don't reach out benevolently, filled with good will for others. You don't seem to care enough. Pain makes you a little person, not a big one, and not a nice one, except perhaps in the case of saints, and I've never known one.

Alice had no sooner gone out, taking that unappetizing tray with her, than Jack tapped at the open door. He looked haggard, but his face lighted when he saw me.

"Well, that's a lot better! You're more like yourself again.

You had us plenty scared last night. That'll larn you to look where you are going. But joking aside, something must be done about those rafters, even if we have to string a row of lights along them." He groped for my hand, felt my pulse. "And you all alone up there."

I remembered the draft that had lifted the loose piece of paper, the creak of a stair. Why, I thought in belated wonder, perhaps this was it, this was the thing I had only half believed. This was the attempt to eliminate me, to clear the way for disposing of Natalie.

I could feel the jolt of my heart and I knew Jack could feel it too. "I'm sorry, Constance. It's a rotten shame. But you're going to be all right now." He looked around as Natalie appeared in the doorway. "Darling, I thought you were going to sleep this morning."

"I slept wonderfully and I feel fine," she said. "The pain-killer worked like a charm, I suppose because I haven't used them in such a long time. I must have slept sixteen hours." She laughed. "I understand that silly Timothy sat up all night, afraid Freda couldn't manage with Constance. I told him to catch up on sleep this morning."

"This," Jack commented in some amusement, "is going to be like one of those enchanted woods where everyone falls asleep: Freda, Joe, Struthers—"

"Well, I'm going to spend the time I usually work with Timothy in putting down all the material Mr. Grace gave me over the telephone yesterday afternoon. A lot of things I never knew and some I'd forgotten. And some very funny ones. It's odd that I'd never have thought of anything about my father as being funny. So I'll be busy, but Alice will be free to sit with you, dear."

"I won't need her," I said. "And there's no reason why I can't handle the mail, not the typing, but at least I can sort out the letters. Oh, and we'll need a lot more stamps."

"She's a little Trojan, isn't she?" Jack said, and Natalie

came to brush her lips across my cheek. Then, as the telephone rang, she said, "I'll take it, Jack. It's high time I came out of that shell and returned to the world." She smiled at me and waited for Jack, who joined her saying, "I'm going back to my workroom. Wait until you see it."

"Freda complains you are moving all the heavy stuff, her rotisserie and crock pot and I don't know what else, down there where she can't get at it."

"Damn! I thought I was making things more convenient."

They both laughed and then Natalie said, in response to the insistent ringing of the telephone, "Yes, yes, I'm coming."

The phone was silenced as she said, "Yes? . . . Oh, Brendon!" There was a long pause. "I think you're taking this too seriously. After all, there's no reason . . . well, if there was an envelope, we couldn't find it . . . Of course, it could have been slipped in the mailbox as a kind of prank. Some youngster . . . Alice? Oh, surely not! That would be too absurd . . . Of course, I'll keep you informed, but let's hope this is the end of the incident. Thank you for your concern."

For a long time I lay staring at the window, trying to reconstruct exactly what had happened to me. One uneasy thought would not be evaded. From the back I might easily have been taken for Natalie. I could remember the flutter of the piece of paper lifted by a draft, the creaking of one of the attic stairs. But that wasn't proof of anything. I might have left the attic door open myself. More significant was the pallor in Freda's face, her haunted expression, her informing Jack that there was no blood on the rafters. Freda who had urged me to go away. Freda who had "promised" Tim that I would be all right, who had left my door open and told me to call loudly if I needed anything. Freda who had stayed on guard all night.

And someone had beaten up Bates. Coincidence? Nonsense. Bates must have seized the first opportunity to attack me and Jack apparently had half killed him for it. Which meant, didn't it, that Jack refused to go along with Bates's ideas? But why had he changed his mind? Bates wanted me out of the way before Natalie was eliminated so that Jack would inherit all and not half of the estate. Jack was against it. I came back to my original conviction that Jack, whatever the plan might be, had grown genuinely devoted to his wife, he was proud of her, he was happy in this new life of his, and he did not want to change it.

But could he control Bates? Could Freda control Bates? Obviously she suspected him of the attack on me and she had made clear to Jack that she knew I had not knocked myself out. Could she, I wondered, have left that warning note for Natalie, afraid to speak openly because of her husband's possible retaliation?

I stirred restlessly and stifled a moan when I shifted position, moving my left leg. In a moment Tim's head popped around the door.

"For heaven's sake," I said crossly, "go back to sleep. I'm all right."

"You were moaning."

"I've got a right to moan if I want to. I like moaning."

He came in to touch my cheek lightly with a fingertip and then he turned my head gently and kissed my mouth. "I'll call the doctor."

Alice stood looking at him, her hands on her hips. "Nice goings-on. Any man in sight."

"Hey," Tim began, but I shook my head at him.

"Doctor's here," Alice said and Tim grinned and went back to his room. In a moment I heard the doctor come up the stairs. He came in, looked me over, and smiled approvingly. "Have a good night?"

"Fine. Most of the time. I only had to take one more of those painkillers."

"Good. I don't like handing out that stuff unless it's necessary." He examined my head, prodded, prepared a fresh dressing that was much smaller and said cheerfully that there wouldn't be a scar. "A bit of luck, that, as you struck the back of your head and then fell forward, gashing your forehead and just missing your eye about half an inch. We can't afford to lose eyes like that."

"I can't afford to lose any eyes," I retorted.

"Well, you're a lot more alive this morning. Let's look at that knee."

After a painful five minutes he nodded in satisfaction. "I see you've already been up. Hurt much?"

"Yes."

"Well, take it easy. You're doing fine, couldn't be better. But keep off the leg as much as you can and if it hurts too much you can have a couple of aspirin. I'll look in sometime tomorrow to check on that gash on your forehead. You were lucky not to do yourself more damage. Now I'll just take a peek at Mrs. Clifford. Electric storms are apt to be bad for her nervous system."

"Oh, she's fine this morning. She came in to see me and she's working now, making some notes for her biography."

He picked up his bag, waved cheerfully at me, and ran down the stairs to let himself out. A moment later I heard his car start up.

There was something so sane and reassuring about the man that I felt completely relaxed, put aside the frightened thoughts I had been harboring, and switched on my little radio, using the earplug so as not to disturb anyone, as long as I was supposed to keep my door open.

Alice clumped up the stairs to drop the morning's mail on the bed and I gathered it up, my hands shaking as I

134

searched for word from my father. There were half a dozen letters in business envelopes and I opened them all, but they urged Natalie to buy leather goods by mail, offered reduced premiums on some kind of health insurance, asked her to subscribe to a clipping bureau that covered all notices of her in the press, and a letter from her Congressman told her what a fine job he was doing.

I went through the other mail, but there was nothing from my father.

About one o'clock Alice stumped in, bringing me a tray containing some canned beef stew, which was only tepid, a hard roll with a pat of butter, and some applesauce.

Natalie came out of her room and I heard Jack calling as she went downstairs. Tim, freshly shaven and looking rested, poked his head in the door and saw my tray.

"Good God! You can't eat that stuff."

"I'm not hungry. At least she couldn't spoil the applesauce."

"Do you like applesauce?"

"No," I admitted.

Tim laughed at that. "Here is where your guardian angel goes off duty," he declared. "I am going to borrow the family car and go out to lunch." He looked at the tray. "A steak," he said thoughtfully, "a baked potato, sliced tomatoes, hot biscuits—"

I moaned.

Jack laughed from the doorway. "Cruel and inhuman treatment. We'll all go out to lunch and bring back something fit for Constance to eat."

"Who is going to look after Kate in the meantime?" Tim demanded.

For a moment the eyes of the two men met and then Jack said smoothly, "Alice can do that."

"I hope she's better as a watchdog than as a cook," Tim said.

Watchdog. So the issue was joined. I thought Jack was going to throw Tim out. Tim was the taller but Jack had more weight and he was in peak condition.

It was Jack who said lightly, "I think we should make Alice eat the stuff on the tray. Serve her right. And she can sit with Constance until we return." He called down, "Darling, we're all going out to lunch. This stuff Alice has prepared isn't fit for a dog."

Natalie laughed. "I'll get my coat. But we must take Timothy along. Anyhow I have some wonderful material for him."

Jack picked up my tray and indicated that Tim was to precede him out of the room. They went down the stairs talking amicably.

II

Fortunately I had the radio as a sort of shield between Alice and me. She sat, rocking vigorously, giving me quick, sidelong looks as though hoping to catch me off guard in some way. I plugged in the earphone and listened to *Sheep May Safely Graze*, and thought how wonderful it would be if Bach had been right about that.

It must have been midafternoon when Jack brought up a glass of sherry, apologized for the delay in getting me something to eat, at which Alice sniffed, but explained that Time and Natalie had been talking so hard that they had sat over their lunch much longer than they intended.

Alice sat firmly in her chair. She had no intention of leaving Jack and me alone. Then Tim appeared, carrying a napkin over his arm, and, with a flourish, presented me with a tray. There was a covered bowl of hot soup, cold sliced turkey, a salad, and a piece of pineapple upside-down cake with whipped cream.

"Good heavens!" I laughed at the amount of food.

"And that," Tim said, "is devotion. If you've ever juggled hot soup and whipped cream in a moving car, you'll know what I've been through. Now eat every bite. I don't intend to move until you do."

At that, Jack, after giving Tim a long hard look, went out of the room and Alice followed. To my surprise Tim reached for my glass of sherry and took a sip. He nodded his head and returned the glass to me.

"Why on earth—"

"Precaution. After all, the kings used to have their tasters. What did they have that you haven't?"

"But, Tim—"

"Drink up and eat up."

He settled in the rocking chair, decided it was too small for him, and moved to the dressing table bench. His eyes rested on the mail. "Any news from your father?"

I shook my head.

"There was barely time to get a reply to you. And you can't expect to hear so soon."

"I suppose not. At least I know he's alive and in New York, just a little over a hundred miles away. It seems almost too good to be true."

"When he gives you an address, I'll drive you down to meet him; that is, as soon as you can be moved."

"The doctor seems to think I'll be fine. No real damage. I just have to go easy with that left leg."

Natalie came in and Tim stood up. She smiled at the inroads I had made on the lunch tray. I had just reached the dessert stage and there was a smear of whipped cream on my upper lip.

"Feeding time at the zoo is nothing compared to it," Tim told her. "When I think what it is going to cost me to feed the woman—"

"To feed—" The lovely eyes moved from Tim to me. "My dear!"

I could feel my face burning. "Don't you believe a word of it."

"You aren't going to marry him?" She was disappointed.

"I don't even know him. Anyhow, he hasn't asked me."

Natalie's lovely laughter made me smile reluctantly. She looked around. "Constance, have you seen my lucky piece? I've looked all over the house for it and gone through everything in our suite at least a dozen times. I've had Jack check the car and call the restaurant. Could I have dropped it in here?"

"I don't know." I described to Tim the four-leaf clover in its plastic case hung on a silver chain. "See if you can find it. It means a lot to Natalie."

"It does indeed. It was Jack's gift to me in his first letter, before I ever saw him. It's always been a kind of omen, as though it was a symbol that he had brought me not only luck but life. As he did, you know."

Tim hunted over the rug and the floor, inch by inch, even lifting the edge of the patchwork quilt and feeling under the edge of the bed. Natalie looked at the rocker and turned over the cushion. At last they gave up.

"I'll look in my room again," she said. "It's probably in a pocket."

"Now that," Tim remarked when she had gone, "is a damned big reaction to the loss of a four-leaf clover."

"It means a lot to her."

"So I gather. Do you intend to treasure any of my gifts like that?"

"I haven't seen any yet," I pointed out, and he laughed.

"Not only greedy but grasping. Let me see your palm." He pretended to study it. "Good God! Nothing but trouble." He bent over, kissed it lightly.

"And why make Natalie think we are in love—or something?"

He grinned widely at that. Then he sobered. "Because,

138

my beloved dumb bunny, Alice is doing her vicious best to make your aunt jealous of you. She thinks you and Clifford have a thing. I'm doing a little undermining."

"Oh," I said flatly. Then I added impulsively, "It must have been Alice—" I explained about the warning note written in red chalk so smeared the handwriting was not identifiable. "Natalie wouldn't let me call the police or tell Jack, but she did let me write Mr. Fowler. I was thinking it was Freda's work but perhaps Alice—"

"For my money that woman's gone over the edge," Tim said. "I don't want any part of her. The sooner I get you away from this combination of neurotics and potential criminals, the better I'll like it."

Apparently Natalie had given up her search for her lucky piece because I could hear Jack reading the paper to her, down in the drawing room, breaking in with comments of his own that aroused her soft laughter.

"Do you think anything can be made of the book?" I asked.

"She gave me some wonderful stuff at lunch. If I were doing my job, I'd be typing notes before I forget them. Her friend Grace seems to be a gold mine. I'd give a lot to have a couple of hours with him. A lot of color and some amusing anecdotes. I can't say old Netherfield is my favorite character, but at least he wasn't dull."

"Why don't you get the stuff down before you forget it?"

"Because Freda is awake at last and bestirring herself about dinner and one look at Alice is enough to give anyone heartburn."

"I don't need anyone."

"That's what you think. Just who do you suppose conked you so neatly over the bean? I looked around the attic. You didn't knock yourself out on a rafter. The only blood is on the corner of a box. It looks to me as though someone hit you on the back of the head. You fell forward, cutting your forehead on the box."

"If anyone hit me, it must have been Bates. I think that's why he was beaten up. Jack didn't like it."

"So he didn't like it. Well, well!"

"Don't look like that, Tim! And you've made fairly clear to Jack that you are suspicious of him. It's a wonder to me he doesn't ask Natalie to throw you out. For heaven's sake, let's forget it for a while." I twisted the dials on the radio, getting rock and roll and commercials and rock and roll and a talk on baby feeding and rock and roll and finally a local station.

The weather, it appeared, was going to be seasonal, which was like a politician being absolutely frank. A gas main had broken, causing considerable damage, but the situation was under control. A man had been found stabbed to death in a cheap rooming house on Railroad Street. According to the owner of the building he had checked in a couple of days before and paid each day in advance. A rule of the house.

"I'll bet," Tim muttered.

The murdered man had registered as Barry Masters and he came to town a couple of times a year. He was the last of his family, all of whom were buried in the local cemetery, and he came to check on their graves. He had not lived in Alcott for twenty years and appeared to have no friends there and no enemies. No reason had been discovered for his murder. His wallet was on the dresser and contained twenty dollars. Apparently he had been stabbed while he lay asleep, his head turned toward the wall, and there was no indication of a struggle.

The chambermaid had not attempted to make up his room until early afternoon because of the DO NOT DISTURB sign on his door, but she had become concerned and had asked the owner to check it out himself.

I switched off the radio. Down below the telephone rang

and Jack answered it. In a moment he called up the stairs, "Struthers! Call for you."

Tim's eyebrows shot up. "Must be Hugh Evans. Only person who knows I am here. I didn't expect any action out of him this soon. I'll be right back."

Through the open door I could hear Natalie and Jack talking in the drawing room. Apparently he said he was going to fix a drink and asked whether she wanted one.

"Can't Bates do it for you?"

"Bates," he told her, "is getting over a hangover."

"Oh, dear, I suppose we'll have to let him go and it's so hard to find a reliable couple any more. And Freda is such a good cook."

If you want Natalie to believe in that hangover, I thought, you'd better keep Bates out of sight until he gets over the effect of the beating; at least, if he looks as bad as Alice says.

Jack went out of the room and I knew he'd have to pass the telephone where Tim was talking, in order to mix his drink.

Tim ended his call abruptly and I heard him accept Jack's offer of a highball. He came back to my room, holding a tall glass, shaking it lightly so the ice tinkled against the side.

"Pleasant sound, isn't it," he said, speaking clearly. He stood close to the bed and caught my wrist in his free hand, looking down at me with the strangest expression on his face. "Not a sound out of you," he said softly. "Not a sound. Clear?"

I nodded.

"That was your father."

Fourteen

When he was sure that I was not going to speak, Tim nodded and pulled the piano bench as close to the bed as possible. Alice was bustling around the hall, trying to appear to busy herself in Natalie's rooms, but actually keeping an eye on Tim and me.

Unexpectedly the somber look in Tim's face faded and he chuckled. "You know, if she thinks I can sweep you off your feet for a little dalliance when you've got a gashed head and a bad leg, she thinks I'm a better man than I am."

"What is it?" I asked quietly.

When Tim made no reply, I said more urgently, but still keeping my voice down, "Is he all right? Why did he ask for you?"

"He didn't want to be identified by asking for you. I'd forgotten what a beautiful voice the man had. It's just the same. He could make the *World Almanac* sound like poetry."

I nodded and tears stung my eyes. Still aware of the open door but with his eyes warningly on me, for fear I'd make some sudden exclamation, Tim said, "You must have said something in your letter to make your father think I was to be trusted. He asked about you but, of course, I had to be evasive. Everything was fine. Something like that. He's quick, isn't he? He asked if I was being overheard and I said probably."

My father had picked up my letter at the GPO and had caught the first bus from the Port Authority Terminal for Alcott.

"Why?"

"He said he didn't like this setup and he wanted you out of here. He—" Tim came to an abrupt halt and I waited. At length he said, "I'm going out to meet him now."

"He'll need money. If you'll look in my purse—it's in the top drawer—there's almost a hundred dollars. Take it to him, please."

Without demur Tim found the purse and handed it to me. I took out the money, which he slipped into his billfold.

"Where are you going to meet him?"

"Tell you later. Anything you need? While I'm gone, keep your door wide open and yell if you have to."

"Bates wouldn't dare try again."

"Wouldn't he? There's a hell of a lot at stake, Kate. For Bates the success of this operation means an easy life, as he'd probably get half the take." He hesitated. "I hate leaving you."

"Tell Freda," I suggested. "I think she knows. She wouldn't let Bates do anything more."

"I'll ask her to keep an eye on you and I won't be gone any longer than I have to."

"I wish to heaven I could go with you! It's maddening to be helpless at a time like this. Tim!"

"Yes?" He turned back from the door.

"Tell him I love him. Tell him not to vanish again. Say —I need him."

"Okay, kid." His eyes were smiling as he went out. I listened, heard him go to his room for a coat, heard him on the stairs, heard him say he needed pipe tobacco and ask if he could pick up anything for anyone, I heard the door close.

And then I waited. Time dragged. Four. Four-thirty.

Four-forty-five. Finally I was looking at my watch every two or three minutes. The early twilight fell. It was almost dark now, but I did not switch on the reading lamp beside the bed. I stared out into the darkness. Automatically the lines came to me, lines I had once heard my father recite when he gave an evening of poetry reading:

> Brightness falls from the air;
> Queens have died, young and fair;
> Dust hath closed Helen's eye.
> I am sick, I must die.
> Lord have mercy on me.

My father was here in Alcott, somewhere close at hand. And, trusting what I had said about Tim, he had sent for him. Why?

At last the car rolled down the driveway past my window and Tim tapped the horn softly. A few minutes later he entered the house.

"Just in time," Jack called cheerfully. "The children's hour is at hand. Bates still seems to be out for the count, so I'm bartender. What's yours?"

"Scotch and water, please."

"I forget what Constance has been drinking."

"Dry martini," Tim said promptly. "A twist of lemon. No ice."

Jack laughed. "Observant, aren't you?"

Natalie joined in the laughter. "My dear, he is planning to be Constance's permanent bartender."

"You don't say! Quick worker, aren't you? Congratulations. Though why she'd look at a guy who talks to her the way you do—"

They were all laughing.

"But you won't take her away now, will you?" Natalie said. "We've had so little time together."

144

"Well, not until after I've gathered more material for the book. Maybe another week will give me enough to get started on. I'll have to get back to California to discuss the new pilot film they are going to make from one of my books and we may combine that with a honeymoon trip. Once we've got a pattern, we can consult by telephone or letter until there is enough in shape so we can get together again about it."

And the dope hasn't even asked me to marry him, I thought furiously. The things he takes for granted! And then my anger died. I remembered that this was only a smoke screen, countering Alice's attempts to arouse Natalie's jealousy of me and Jack.

Tim emphasized this by remarking with a laugh, "Thank God for television. When you've got it made, it really pays. Looks as though I'd be able to keep my girl in style."

And that, I thought, takes me out of Natalie's will without any pain. I felt a surge of relief followed by dismay. Then what about Natalie? I couldn't, just for my own safety, go away and leave her to the mercies of Bates and Jack. Bates was the stronger of the two. Jack might be able to beat him up but it was Bates who called the turns.

Warn Natalie? I couldn't watch the glow of happiness fade from her face, from her life. I'd tell Mr. Fowler what I knew and what I suspected. I'd write to him in the morning. Somehow, some way, he would manage to protect Natalie. He loved her. Perhaps he was the only person who really loved her, that beautiful, charming, gifted woman with her warm generosity. It was an odd thought. Her public probably thought that she was surrounded by admirers.

Tim set down a tray holding a highball and a martini glass. There was also a plate of canapés: olives, celery stuffed with cheese, anchovies on toast bits.

"Courtesy of the house," he said in his resonant voice. He handed me the martini, smiling into my anxious eyes. He lifted his glass.

There was a moment's silence and then he exclaimed, "This is not the children's hour; it's a wake! We need cheering up." He turned on the radio, found a station playing *Swan Lake*, and then crouched beside the bed, keeping his voice low, the music covering it.

He had met my father in the local drugstore and they had gone to the place where we had had the hot rum punch. My father, he meant, though he said only "he," had changed a lot. He was older, his hair was white, he was a lot thinner. "But, darling, he's *all right.*" As I looked my question, he said, "He refused a drink and ordered coffee instead. He hasn't touched a drink for more than a year. Through a friend he got a job in New York, training young actors, coaching people, and making enough to live on. He returned the money to you though I thought, for a moment, he was going to break down. He's come all the way back except for regaining his confidence. We're going to give him that."

"Oh, Tim!"

I could hear the joy in my voice but there was no answering pleasure in Tim's. It was bleak.

"He came up here, as I said, on the first bus but he didn't know how to get in touch with you without revealing his identity."

"Why shouldn't he?"

"I'm coming to that." Something in his voice silenced me. I set down my glass with a shaking hand so that some of the cocktail splashed over on the tray.

"He decided to wait until today to reach you, so he found a cheap rooming house and got something to eat at a diner. He was tired and worried and he went to bed and slept heavily. There was no one around when he got up this morning and only one other roomer, who had a DO NOT DISTURB sign on his door."

Tim's eyes warned me before I could make a sound. My heart began to leap like a jumping bean.

"He went out, got some breakfast, strolled around the town and even walked past this house. He said it seemed to be much the same except the trees were higher and a small girl with pale hair and blue eyes wasn't in it any more." Tim went on gently, "He loved your mother, kid."

"I know."

"And he loves you. Which reminds me." Tim set down his glass, leaned over to pull me into his arms and kiss me. "He sent his love. I told him—I thought it might reassure him—that I loved you too."

"Tim! You're telling me my—he—was in the room next to the man who was murdered."

"Yes." He put the glass back in my hand and I sipped it slowly, feeling its warmth go through me.

"It was a—mistake, wasn't it?"

Tim didn't ask what I meant. He knew. "Well, there seemed to be no possible reason why anyone would kill a poor guy who didn't even know anyone in Alcott. He came here just to visit the cemetery, for God's sake!"

"So—" I took another sip. "I've always believed someone was sabotaging my father's career. Someone meant him to die last night. Someone got the wrong man. That's the way it was?"

Tim shrugged. "I think so. You think so. He thinks so. When he heard about the murder—"

"How did he know about it?"

"In the drugstore. A couple of cops were having coffee at the fountain, talking about it. They're interested in the guy in the next room, who registered as Edwin Booth."

"Oh, how foolish of him!"

"Well, he didn't know at the time, of course, that there was going to be a murder and that the name would be called into question. What gets me is how anyone knew he was coming here and that he was staying at that rooming house."

"There's the letter I lost, the one I'm sure Bates got hold of."

"But that didn't mention coming here."

"It mentioned General Delivery. If someone was waiting and followed him—"Where is—he—now?"

"That's what took me so long. I drove him to Danbury to get a bus back to New York. There was quite a crowd getting on and no one was likely to notice him. In another hour he'll be safe at home. There's no reason on earth why anyone should ever associate him with the elusive Edwin Booth."

"Of all the—"

"Okay, it was a stupid thing to do, but he didn't know. How could he?"

"But now the dead man has been identified, there will be a real search for the missing Edwin Booth, won't there? And the one who tried to kill him will try again. Won't he? Won't he?"

"Don't wave that glass around, Kate. You've spilled half your drink. I'm not going down to mix you another. With my lofty reputation I can't afford to have an inebriated wife."

"Oh—"

He stood up as Natalie came in, holding an untouched glass in her hand. Tim switched off the radio. Then, with an exclamation of concern, he took her arm and eased her

148

gently into the rocking chair. She was colorless and her hands were shaking. He took the glass out of her hand and set it on the tray.

"Natalie!" I exclaimed, sitting bolt upright and then wincing as I twisted my leg. "What's wrong?"

For a moment I thought she wasn't going to speak at all. Then she moistened her lips and said, her voice almost a croak, "There's another one."

"Another what?"

"I came up—I wanted to talk to you and Tim—I was so happy to think of you falling in love like that—just the way Jack and I did—and I stopped in my room to put on some lipstick and powder and I—found—this."

She held the grubby piece of paper to me. This too was printed in red chalk. "It was—just—lying there."

I thought for a moment she was going to faint, and Tim, who had been watching her closely, lifted her glass to her lips, steadied her hand and her head and made her swallow a few sips.

"Okay," he said quietly. "It's okay, Mrs. Clifford. Now what—"

I read the note aloud:

You haven't much time left. Make the most of it. I can't protect you any longer.

A friend.

Without asking Natalie's permission, I passed the note on to Tim, who took it carefully by one corner. "What did you do with the other one?" He sounded so matter-of-fact that we both stared at him in surprise.

Natalie gestured mutely to me, but the color was beginning to come back into her lips. Tim pressed the glass into her hand again and this time she drank more and seemed to be getting back some control.

"I sent it to Mr. Fowler," I told him.

"He telephoned," Natalie said. "He was horribly upset. I absolutely refused to let him call in the police. It would provide a newsmen's holiday. I've thought of everything: a child's prank, some outsider slipping the first letter in the mailbox. But this one was just lying on my dressing table. At first I didn't pay any attention. I assumed it was a handkerchief I had dropped. One thing sure," and her voice began to rise with a touch of incipient hysteria, "tomorrow I'm going to the city to get some glasses. It's absurd to refuse to wear them just for vanity. And all that pain. This way I'm helpless, groping in the dark, I can't see what's going on around me."

"Stop it!" Tim said so sharply that she gasped.

Then she gave her lovely smile and lifted her glass. "Sorry. I don't often go off the beam this way. But there was an occultist who warned me of danger. He saw a knife, and then I lost my lucky piece."

She broke down, crying in great gasping sobs like a small child, uninhibited, completely out of control.

Tim looked at me in dismay. This was more than he could handle. Almost simultaneously Jack came leaping up the stairs and Alice ran from the Cliffords' suite. Jack knelt beside Natalie, trying to take her in his arms.

"No!" she cried, completely beside herself. "No!"

And then Alice pushed him away. "You come with Alice and I'll tuck you up and give your back a good rub and fix you a glass of hot milk and you'll be right as rain in the morning." She turned to glare at me. "Why couldn't you let her alone? I knew from the first you were a troublemaker."

"No," Natalie said as Alice drew her unresistingly out of her chair and led her toward the door. "No, Constance. Please stay. Don't go away. Please don't go away, you and Timothy. Please stay. Please!"

150

Jack got slowly to his feet. "What's wrong with her? What's wrong? Anyone would think she was afraid of me. What caused it?"

"She got another anonymous letter," Tim told him.

"Another—"

"A printed note without an envelope. She found it on her dressing table just now."

"I—see." Jack looked challengingly at Tim. "That's what you were getting at yesterday. You think I hurt Constance. You think I'd hurt Natalie. What in hell's name is wrong? Anyone would assume I'm a mass murderer."

"I've said so from the beginning," Alice snapped as she came into the room. "I've got her on her bed now and she's not to be disturbed. But does anyone care? No, the men all gather around Miss Armstrong, sitting in her bedroom. And what I'd like to know is what you were doing, snooping around in the attic when you knocked yourself out?"

"I went up because my aunt told me nothing was ever thrown away and I might find the recording of my mother's Town Hall debut there."

Alice's lips twitched. "Did you find it?"

"I found it with all her clothes. Just tossed into a box, and the record had been ruined, cut with a knife."

"I did that," Alice said. "And good riddance." There was malevolence in her eyes as she went back to Natalie's room.

"Good God!" Jack exclaimed. "The woman is mad. I don't know why I didn't realize that before. I just thought she was abnormally protective of Natalie. But I believed I had set Natalie free of all that need for protection. I should never have let Alice go with us."

He looked at Tim, met an unrevealing face, turned to me. "Constance, this is God's truth. I love Natalie. I think she's the loveliest, the most marvelous human being I ever knew. The most brilliant. Way beyond me. I know that. But if I could spare her anything, I'd do it at any cost to myself.

151

Living with her has been a revelation. I've never known what happiness was before. I'm going to fight to keep it."
He went out. Tim had gone to the window and was looking down the driveway. Then he gave a sharp exclamation.

"He's headed for the apartment over the garage. God help Bates!"

"We can't just let something happen, Tim."

"I'm not man enough to tackle them both."

"Get Freda."

He half laughed. "You think she's a better man than I am?"

"She won't want anything to happen to Bates, though heaven knows why."

"Be seeing you." Tim gave me a hasty kiss and ran down the stairs.

Fifteen

Tim warned Freda that Jack was on the warpath and she'd better take a hand. He said the sooner she told Bates the facts of life, the better. And he suggested she make clear to both of them the game was up. Freda, he reported, had raced out to the garage without waiting to get a coat.

"I hung around the bar and mixed myself a quick one," he said, "until I saw Jack and Freda coming back together. I figured the situation was under control, so I came up here."

"Who do you think wrote those notes? It has to be someone in the house."

"Of course it's either Freda or Alice. My money is on Alice. That woman won't be happy until she's swept all of us under the rug. Now tell me about the destruction of your mother's recording. That was sheer viciousness, Kate."

I told him of finding the box into which my mother's belongings had been tossed, even a magnificent sable coat, and how the record had been mutilated.

He listened as though weighing it against some other facts and nodded. "No wonder Natalie tends to have hysterical attacks with that half-demented woman constantly feeding her poison. It's a wonder to me she doesn't break altogether."

"Jack wants to send Alice away."

"Natalie will never allow it. She is far more under Alice's influence than she is under Clifford's. Anyhow, Alice may actually be Natalie's best protection. Who's to know?"

We heard Jack come up the stairs and open the door to Natalie's room, heard Alice utter some sort of protest, and then Jack apparently picked her up bodily, put her out in the hall, and locked the door.

"Take it easy," Tim said softly. "This is between husband and wife. We can't interfere."

"But—"

"Look, use your head. Jack wouldn't dare hurt her when he is known to be alone with her. She's safe enough now."

"But if Alice didn't write those warning notes—"

"Then it must be Freda, who can't control her husband but wants to help Natalie if she can."

The two-toned doorbell rang and Freda went to answer it. Apparently the maid was up in her attic room. A pleasant voice asked to see Mrs. Clifford. She wasn't, Freda said, seeing anyone.

"She'll see me," the man said confidently. "I'm leaving for Arizona in the morning and this is the only chance I'll have to talk to her." He sneezed. "It's as important for her as it is for me. Tell her it's Mr. Grace."

Tim got up in a hurry and went to call down the stairs, "Please come in, Mr. Grace. If Mrs. Clifford isn't up to seeing you, there are a lot of questions I'd like to ask you. My name's Struthers. I'm doing Mrs. Clifford's biography."

"Oh. Glad to talk to you."

The voices had been loud and clear, particularly Tim's, and Jack opened Natalie's door. "Mr. Grace? My wife will be delighted to see you and hopes you'll dine with us. I'll fix you a drink while she is changing. She hasn't been well."

"I'm sorry to hear that."

154

Jack ran down the stairs, greeted the newcomer, and said, "Freda, another place for Mr. Grace."

Then I heard Natalie call, "Two extra places, please. Jack, you and Tim can carry Constance downstairs. It will be so much nicer."

She stood in my doorway, smiling and supervising my chair lift on the men's linked hands down the stairs to the drawing room where Mr. Grace was standing before the fireplace, a tall glass in his hand. He was the most nondescript man I'd ever seen—size, weight, coloring, features, all completely average. Not one distinguishing quality about him except for a red nose explained by a particularly violent cold.

Natalie held out her hand, smiling. "How good of you to come," she said with all her customary graciousness and no indication of the state of collapse in which she had been so short a time before, except that the great eyes seemed to have sunken in her head and even the most discreet use of rouge had only accentuated her deep pallor.

The conversation was idle. Natalie carried most of the burden, discussing the changes in Alcott since he had written his book and lamenting that no copy was to be had.

Jack answered the telephone and called Tim, who did a little talking and a lot of listening. Once he said dryly, "Sounds like a regular procession." After a longer pause he asked sharply, "Sure about that?" At length he said, "Not as surprised as you'd think. I've had a kind of hunch . . . Damned right it means trouble . . . I don't know how to handle it. Sorry you're disappointed."

The housemaid had to serve dinner as apparently Bates was still not fit to be seen, much too battered to put in an appearance.

Natalie got to her feet smiling. "Bring your drinks with you," she said. "We're shorthanded tonight and Freda is afraid her dinner will spoil."

Tim settled me awkwardly at the table, with a stool under my knee so I wouldn't have to bend it. All through dinner I was aware that he and Jack were conscious of each move the other made, though Tim was apparently devoting all his attention to Mr. Grace, endeavoring to get some information from him about the Netherfield family. He didn't get far. Mr. Grace's cold had reached such proportions that he was capable of nothing but sneezing, trumpeting into a handkerchief, and coughing. He spread enough germs around him to infect us all, I thought indignantly.

Freda's dinner, as usual, was beyond praise. Petite marmite, a roast of lamb with mint sauce, creamed potatoes, green peas and a tossed salad. Tiny hot rolls had already been placed on the butter plates. The maid served awkwardly, but no one had any complaints.

"I hope you'll let us put you up for the night," Jack said. "It's a long drive back to New York and there's plenty of room. Anyhow I know Natalie and Mr. Struthers will be anxious to get a lot of information out of you."

"Thank you, I'd appreciate that. I drove up a couple of nights ago in the midst of a terrific storm. I'd have called sooner but I had to do some checking on old archives at the library, which took longer than I expected."

"I suppose the village has changed a lot since your time."

"More action, anyhow," Grace said with a laugh. "Man stabbed to death in a rooming house while he slept. Queer deal. No one can figure it. No enemies. Stranger in town. Seems he was an old-timer from way back, so I went around to take a look on the chance I could identify him. Never saw the guy before. It was an outside chance, of course. They had all his belongings laid out—clothes, wallet, and some queer thing that had been tangled in the blanket. Nothing that would be easy to trace."

He began to cough, a cough that went on and on. Then he said, "Sorry, my dear. I guess that ends any talk tonight.

156

Talking is contraindicated in my case. I'm heading for Phoenix in the morning. Cold weather is not for me and I got pretty wet in that storm the other night."

He turned to me. "Looks as though you'd run into some trouble too."

"I knocked myself out on a low rafter in the attic," I said, "and fell, throwing my knee out. I'm practically well now except for walking and I expect to do that in the morning."

"Speaking of morning," Grace said to Natalie, "as I'll be off to an early start, probably before you are awake, can you let me have that list of addresses we were discussing?"

"Addresses?" she said vaguely. Then she added, "Oh, of course. Constance, will you pour the coffee while I go up to my room?"

This time, leaning heavily on Tim's arm and sort of hopping, I made it on my own feet into the drawing room and took Natalie's big chair near the fireplace with the coffee tray on a table in front of me. I poured and Tim served the after-dinner coffee, while Jack served brandy and Grace talked about Phoenix.

"Nice place for a man with bad lungs," he said, "but it takes money to live there."

"It takes money everywhere," Jack said grimly.

In a few minutes Natalie came down and handed Grace an envelope. "I think these are the ones you wanted."

He slipped it into his pocket. "Thanks a lot." He began to cough again. "Sorry, but I guess I'll have to say good night. The best of luck to your book, Struthers. You have a fine subject. Later, when I get on my feet, I'll try to help you out with what I know."

He shook hands briskly with Jack, pressed Natalie's hand, and followed Jack up to the room next to mine. I heard them chat for a moment, and Jack called Alice and told her to make up the bed and went down to get a night-cap for his guest.

"Sorry to cause you all this trouble," Grace said.

"I'm getting used to it," Alice said with her usual graciousness. "Strangers all over the place. Come and go even when Mrs. Clifford is almost too tired to get out of bed. Just wearing her out, the lot of you."

The voices had been loud and clear.

"Oh, dear!" Natalie exclaimed, appalled. "Alice is really—"

"Really," Jack said grimly. He went up the stairs and I heard him say, "Alice, you will apologize to Mr. Grace for your discourtesy. And don't let it happen again. Understand?"

There was an awkward silence and Natalie bit her lips, looking at me in dismay. "She's always been so loyal, so devoted, but I don't know what to do about her."

"Leave her to Clifford," Tim suggested. "Until you've heard her rip into Kate, you haven't heard anything."

"Oh, my dear, I'm so sorry! You should have told me. She is really getting very odd."

Alice came stumping down the stairs and went back to the kitchen and her own dinner. Before the door closed, I heard her say to Freda in her own inimitable way, "I hope your husband will be fit to be seen tomorrow."

Jack came down and smiled at his disturbed wife. "It's all right, darling. Leave Alice to me. I'll straighten her out if it's the last thing I do."

"She's taken such good care of me, Jack."

"She's tried to imprison you, my darling. If she had her own way, you'd never see another living soul. She's like your father in that way, from what I can make out. And she gets worse."

This was a domestic matter and I glanced at Tim, who nodded, said, "Time you went back to bed," picked me up in his arms without ceremony, and carried me upstairs. Mr. Grace was standing beside his bed. He had ripped open the envelope Natalie had given him and he was smiling. When he saw us, he beamed, said good night, and closed his door.

Tim set me down on the side of the bed. "Can you undress yourself or shall I call Alice?"

"I can manage. Tim, was that my father you were talking to?"

"No," he said slowly, "but the call was about your father."

"What do you mean?"

"That was Hugh Evans. At my request he was watching the GPO when your father arrived to pick up his letter, and Hugh wasn't the only one. Bates was there and a man who sounds like a dead ringer for this guy Grace."

"But—"

"Your father and Bates and Hugh Evans all took the bus up to Alcott. Grace apparently drove because there was a yellow Volkswagen at the bus stop when it reached here. Raining like hell and a bad electric storm. Your father inquired and then went to the rooming house, which is the only one in town. Hugh and Bates trailed along and Hugh says he picked up a nasty cold. The Volkswagen brought up the rear. Hugh says your father got room 208 and the poor devil who was stabbed had room 206. Bates went on home. It's my guess that Grace slept in his car and it's no wonder he picked up that cold."

"All those people trailing my father! All of them can identify him and he doesn't have an alibi. Oh, dear God!"

"He may have no alibi, but he has no motive either. Just remember that."

"But Bates and the man Grace—why is everyone acting so oddly?"

"Let me go on with this saga. Hugh slipped into the library at closing time and hid behind the stacks. He spent the night there. It was when he dropped into a diner next day that he heard of the murder. He went at once to the

159

temporary morgue in the basement of the Town Hall and was relieved to find the man was not your father. They told him he was the second man to inquire."

"Both Bates and Grace expected it would be my father, didn't they?"

"Who else? What gets me is why Grace told that story tonight. It isn't dinner table conversation."

"But why is he acting like this? What association has he with my father?"

"If I told you what I suspect, you'd think I am crazy."

"But no one hated my father."

"Oh, yeah? Alice did for one. She's made that clear over and over. I'm going out to call Hugh. I have a job for him in the morning."

"That's your specialty, isn't it?"

"What is?"

"Finding a solution for unsolved murders. That's what brought you here."

"Yes."

"I can't bear it if you smash up Natalie's happiness, Tim. She's had only one year out of all her life. You can't destroy that."

"I have a job to do, Kate; not always a pleasant job; and when it involves people I know, it's a grim job."

"But that won't stop you?"

"It won't stop me. And there's one good thing in all this. Your father took the Danbury bus but no one trailed him home."

"What does it matter? They know who he is. And yet they can't possibly believe he would kill an unknown man. In fact, they expected him to be the victim."

"Practically anyone can believe six impossible things before breakfast. Now I'm going into my own room and make an impressive racket on the typewriter. Good old Struthers

160

on the job. Then I'll slide out and call Hugh. But first lock your door."

I half expected that he would kiss me, but he just stood waiting until I limped over to the door, shut it in his face, and locked it.

Sixteen

Next morning was a belated Indian summer with a clear sky and a blazing sun. But the air was crisp and had a bite in it. After breakfast, which Freda brought up to me on a tray, a raddled Freda with twitching lips and eyes that were too bright, I managed to dress. I couldn't risk a shower or a tub bath for fear of falling, but I got into my clothes carefully, except for bad luck with pantyhose. Each time I tried to bend my knew, I ripped the nylon until I was down to my last pair.

I stopped at Natalie's open door and looked into her sitting room. She was lying on the chaise longue and again wearing a lovely housecoat, this one of nile green velvet, but the color was trying and seemed to make her skin almost gray. She lifted her hand in a little gesture of welcome and I went in.

The mail was scattered over the three-legged table she had pulled across her lap and she was bending over it, holding her little reading glass.

"Let me do that," I said.

She gave me her lovely smile, as I limped toward her. "The halt and the blind."

"Not so much halt today. I feel wonderful except I didn't risk a tub or a shower and I ripped my hose trying to get them over my lame knee without bending it."

She pushed the untidy stack of letters toward me and

leaned back for a moment with her hand over her eyes. "These headaches are enough to drive me mad."

"You shouldn't have tried to read those letters when it causes you such eyestrain."

"It's vanity," she admitted. "Jack loves my eyes. I hate having to hide them behind ugly glasses."

"But only when you're reading. You could do that in the strict privacy of your room."

"You're such a nice child and your Timothy is nice too. Isn't it strange that it should happen to us both, in the same way and in the same house? You are like me in lots of ways. When we fall in love, we just go overboard."

I tried to laugh but somehow it wasn't really funny, pretending to Natalie that Tim was in love with me, when he was only building a smoke screen.

"And it's nice to know he's so successful," Natalie went on, much to my surprise. "Jack says people make simply fabulous sums when a television series makes a hit, like *All in the Family* and the Lucy shows. Not that I think money is essential for happiness, but you can feel sure Timothy doesn't—he won't expect—you can just sit back in comfort and not worry."

So Natalie had begun to wonder about Jack's devotion, about his money, about his lack of ambition. There I suspected Fowler of watering the seed Alice had planted. How long could a marriage last without trust?

There was nothing I could say. I glanced casually over the mail. There wasn't so much this morning, not more than a dozen letters.

"There wasn't one of those printed ones today," Natalie said. "That's what I was looking for. Another warning note. Oh, I hear Timothy. Heavens, what a lot of noise the boy makes when he moves a chair or shuts a door. You run along and see what you can do with those letters. As soon as I've been fitted for glasses, I intend to answer them properly myself. Good morning, Timothy! Heavens, how aggressively cheerful you look this morning!"

"My first sight of my bride-to-be," Tim declared, "always affects me like that." Impudently he bent over and kissed me full on the lips, smiling into my furious eyes. "Now, ma'am," he said to Natalie, "I'll be as gloomy as you like."

"Heaven forbid!" she laughed. "Well, where do we start? Oh, Constance, you've dropped a letter."

Tim bent to scoop it up, stood looking at it. There was no envelope.

"Is it—" Natalie asked, her voice shaking.

"Yes, it's one of them there." Tim read it aloud:

> I can't give you another warning. Things have gone too far. I am sorry.
>
> Your friend.

He put the paper into her reaching fingers. "Your hand is like ice!" he exclaimed.

Natalie stared at the note, but I don't think she really saw it. "Constance, you remember what I said about my lucky piece? It brought me life and its loss would bring me death."

"Natalie!"

She waved a protesting hand. "Run along. I'm just upset." As there was the sound of a chair moving in Jack's bedroom, she called impatiently, "Oh, don't hover, Alice! I don't need a watchdog. Anyhow, Mr. Struthers is here. Go away at once!" She waited impatiently until Alice slammed out of Jack's room and went downstairs, muttering. Then she took a long breath, trying to pull herself together. "All right. Let's get to work."

"Too bad Mr. Grace was too ill to give us any information," Tim said. "I didn't see him at breakfast so I assume he's on his way."

"Yes, he's headed for Arizona. Jack's working down in that shop he is building in the basement and Bates has finally been persuaded to wash the car. If Freda weren't such a divine cook, I'd get rid of them both."

"You might do worse." Tim added with a long-suffering sigh, "If my bride-to-be would kindly get the hell out of this room, I could sit down for a change. Always the gentleman."

"Why do you put up with it?" Natalie asked, laughing.

"It's that romantic touch, that chivalry, that clank of armor as the knight rides to the rescue."

He took a menacing step toward me and I limped out of the room. The housemaid had already done Tim's room and she was working in mine.

"Am I in your way?" she asked.

"No, I'm going to use Mr. Struthers's typewriter."

"Queer about that man who got murdered, isn't it?" the maid commented.

I stopped short. "Is there anything new? I haven't seen a paper or listened to the radio."

"My grandfather remembers the whole family, very united they were, and this was the only one left. He comes —he came up twice every year to make sure their graves were well-cared-for and to put in plants and leave fresh flowers and all like that. Not an enemy in the world, you'd think. And stabbed in his sleep. Not even a fair fight. It don't seem right. I hope they catch that Edwin Booth. They're really spreading a net for him, at least that's what my uncle says and he's on the State Police. They got a theory—" She broke off abruptly. "Sorry. Uncle Max always warns me not to repeat anything I hear." She bent over and pulled a sheet tight on my bed. Reluctantly I went into Tim's room and sorted the letters. Except for a couple of glowing pieces of fan mail, which I put aside to please Natalie, there was nothing important. I opened the typewriter and saw the envelope slipped under the platen. It was addressed to Miss Constance Armstrong.

Report from the mastermind. Hugh called early this morning. He's been digging on Grace, which was easy. Grace is a private investigator, at least that's what it says in the telephone book and on his office door. Out of town for a couple of days, according to his office girl.

Last night I took a quick look at Natalie's desk. What she put in that envelope for Grace wasn't a list of addresses. It was a check for $25,000. This is my idea of a damned big fee, or signs of a black man under the lumber. Is she on to Jack? And/or Bates?

Watch yourself, Kate. We're closing in and there's apt to be bad trouble. Don't take any chances and don't trust anyone—except me, of course. If you weren't so thickheaded and stubborn, I'd drag you out of here by the hair of the head, but I know you won't go until you are sure Natalie is safe.

One thing I've been holding out on you—I love you.

Tim

II

Once I had stopped mooning like an idiot over Tim's letter, though as a first love letter it was a washout from any point of view, it seemed to me a professional writer could have done better. All that bride-to-be stuff and the public

166

kiss had been for Natalie to report to Jack, meaning, "See? Constance doesn't need anything from me except maybe a wedding present." And Jack would let things ride. He didn't want to give up a life that had provided him with something he'd never known before, harmony and comfort and gracious living at its best, and a beautiful wife who adored him. He needn't go farther. He needn't take any more risks.

The only risk was Joe Bates. He could have left those warning notes in Natalie's suite. But why rattle before he struck? That was the perplexing thing. Why any warning at all? So that left Alice and Freda.

The elusive Mr. Grace was not an historian who had written about Alcott and the Netherfields. He was a private investigator who had been checking on my father and had followed him from the GPO in New York to Alcott and had gone to the morgue to look at the body of the man who had been stabbed to death.

The more I considered the whole mess, the less sense I made of it. The infuriating thing was that Tim had, or thought he had, the essential clue.

The housemaid had said that a wide net was being spread for the missing Edwin Booth, but Grace and Bates must both know his identity. They had been waiting for him to pick up my letter. Bates had known because he had found my father's letter. But how had Grace known?

I forced myself to settle down and answer letters, putting aside the two that Natalie would enjoy. A writer has to be awfully blasé not to feel a kind of inward glow over letters from people who have liked his books enough to write about them.

There wasn't much to do. I sealed the letters, stamped them, closed Tim's typewriter and, with his letter to me securely fastened inside my bra—this one I intended to keep—I went down, leaning on the banister to take as much weight as possible off my lame knee, to put the letters in the basket for outgoing mail under the mailbox, and drifted back to the kitchen.

Freda, Alice, the maid and Bates were all sitting around the kitchen table drinking coffee and eating fresh gingerbread, which scented the air, as it had probably just come out of the oven.

I can't say I felt welcome but I sniffed and said, "Oh, that smells good!" As this did not bring any response, I tried again. "I came down hoping there'd be some coffee, just instant if you haven't anything else—" The big coffeepot was in plain sight.

Yielding to pressure, Bates got up to pull out a chair, Freda cut me a slice of flaky gingerbread and put a pat of butter on the plate, and the maid poured the coffee. Only Alice ignored my presence. In fact that day I noticed the change in her. Where she had resented me before, now she looked as though she hated me.

It was Freda who finally broke the awkward silence by saying brightly, "I hear you're to be congratulated, Miss Armstrong. Joe says Mr. Clifford told him you are going to marry Mr. Struthers."

I smiled noncommittally.

Freda tried again. "Quite a romance!"

This goaded Alice into speech. "Like your mother in more ways than one. She upped and married your father before he had a chance to look at another woman."

The maid gasped and Freda protested. "Alice!"

If Tim hadn't had a chance to look at another woman in twenty-eight years, then he wasn't the man I thought he was. In my most ladylike manner I wanted, more than anything, to slap Alice's malicious, lying mouth. Instead I said what I thought would hurt her most. "I hope I'll be like my mother in being so loved and having such a happy marriage. If you could have seen the women who envied

168

her, and my father never even looked at them."

And so much for you, I thought, at my sweetest and most feminine, or perhaps I mean feline. I'd never before been aware of my claws, but they were all out now.

"George Armstrong," Alice said, her face a mottled red with fury. I sipped the coffee, tasted the gingerbread and gave Freda a look of appreciation at which she beamed, though she was as tense as a tightwire, she almost vibrated with tension. Only the maid and I were comparatively calm and even she was aware of the atmosphere. She finished her coffee hastily and said she still had the drawing room to do.

"George Armstrong," Alice repeated when the maid had gone, or rather made her escape. "Quite an actor in his day. I always wondered what became of him. That's the way it is with a lot of them. Here today and gone tomorrow."

"Like Mr. Grace," I said idly. "He certainly cut his visit short." I pushed back my chair. "Thanks for the coffee and the gingerbread, Freda. Like everything you make, it was wonderful. Well, thank heaven, it's not raining. I have to go to the shopping center and get some pantyhose. With this darned leg I managed to rip every pair I own except the ones I have on."

"You mustn't walk on that bad leg," Bates said abruptly. "The doctor wanted you to keep off it as much as possible. I haven't anything special to do. I'll run you down. Won't take any time at all."

I didn't like it. I didn't like it at all. I tried to tell myself that he wouldn't dare do anything to me, not when his wife and Alice knew he was with me. I went up to my room for my coat and, on impulse, scrawled a hasty note to Tim, saying that Bates was going to drive me to the shopping center and I should be back in thirty minutes at the outside.

When I came downstairs, Bates already had the car at the curb. Before I could get in, there were running steps and

Freda, hastily pulling on a coat, came out to climb into the front seat beside her glowering husband. She had not even taken off her apron.

"I just remembered I'm all out of wool for that sweater I'm knitting," she explained. She went on, overdoing it as people are apt to do when they try to bolster up an unlikely story. "The cost of a really good sweater these days! Just sky-high. It's cheaper to make them yourself, I always say."

"How about lunch?" Bates asked.

"It may be a little late, but it won't take so long. Curried lamb from the leftover roast and I've already made the curry. Just have to heat it up. And instant rice takes no time at all. And I made a jellied vegetable salad this morning."

Bates sulked and, because he was in a bad temper, he drove carelessly, nearly sideswiping a car so that Freda clutched at his arm and cried, "Joe! Watch what you are doing."

He swallowed what he was about to say and switched on the radio. After the inevitable dose of rock and roll a brisk voice said, "The search for the missing Edwin Booth has been extended to six states. Lieutenant Carver of the State Police said today that, since no apparent reason has been discovered for the murder of the actual victim, it is conceivable that the wrong man was killed and the real victim was intended to be Edwin Booth. It is possible that the name is not his own and that he might be a member of a gang, who was followed here. The numbers on the doors of the two rooms, 206 and 208, are difficult to make out in the inadequately lighted hallway. Mr. Booth is urged, for his own safety, to report to the police at once.

"All that is known of Mr. Booth is that he arrived in Alcott on the New York bus in the late evening, and left the following morning. No clues were found in his room and he had carried only a worn briefcase instead of a suitcase. He did not take the New York bus and any motorist picking up a hitchhiker early yesterday morning is urged to report at once.

"According to the lodging house owner, Booth was about six feet tall, white hair, thin face, wore amber-tinted glasses, a dark suit and a blue pullover with a V neck and a short storm coat. His age is estimated at roughly fifty-five to sixty and he was haggard as though he might be recuperating from an illness. Mental institutions report no patients missing. The search at present is being concentrated in New York City, from where he took the bus to Alcott.

"In case he has not left the village, citizens are urged to report seeing such a man, to make sure their houses and cars are securely locked. Remember that the killer—if he is the killer—is dangerous and he is armed with a knife."

Bates switched off the radio. "What do you think, Joe?" Freda asked. "It's a queer case, isn't it, when they don't know which man was supposed to be killed and whether this Booth was the killer or the intended victim."

"Yeah," Bates said.

"Edwin Booth," Freda said thoughtfully. "That name seems familiar, but I don't remember meeting anyone of that name. Do you?"

"His brother assassinated President Lincoln," Bates said. "Booth himself was an actor. You should remember that from your history book."

"Oh, well, it could hardly be him, could it?"

"God, but you're stupid!" Bates said.

Freda was too accustomed to her husband's rotten manners to be disturbed. "Well, I couldn't help wondering. If it isn't the man's real name, it makes him seem more suspicious, doesn't it? And why use a famous name?"

"Probably an actor," Bates said. "Who else would think of using such a name?" He chuckled. "Some lousy actor."

171

Seventeen

I thought for a while that Freda was going to stick to me like a burr in the shopping center, but I discovered what I wanted in a few minutes and she got involved in matching wool. I wandered around the counter, hightailed it out of the store, and ran to the drugstore, where I found an empty telephone booth and called Mr. Fowler. I got him after going through the hands of three obstructive women.

"So you're in New York, Constance," he said in a tone of satisfaction when I finally reached him. "Suppose you plan to meet me for lunch and we'll get you settled somewhere right away."

"I'm in Alcott, Mr. Fowler, but I've got a lot to tell you." I poured out everything I knew, with the exception of my father's arrival in Alcott and the murder of the man in the next room. I described the three warning letters without envelopes left in Natalie's private sitting room. I told him about Mr. Grace, who was supposed to be an authority on the Netherfield family but who was really a private investigator to whom Natalie had paid twenty-five thousand dollars.

"Good God!" Fowler exclaimed.

And then I told him that Tim's real reason for coming to the house had been to find out whether Jack was the man who had persuaded Gertrude Evans to leave him two hundred thousand dollars, cutting out her nephew, her only

172

living relative. She had been killed shortly after making her will by a hit-run driver.

I reported the talk I had overheard between Jack and Bates, the latter insisting on the original plan going through, the former saying it had been changed. I dropped in more coins, looking through the glass door of the telephone booth to make sure Bates wasn't hovering around, and said Tim believed Jack was holding out until I could be eliminated and they could collect the whole amount instead of only fifty percent when Natalie—when Natalie—

I swallowed hard, caught my breath, and rushed on. "And Tim has told Natalie that he and I are going to be married at once and go away and he is going to make a huge amount of money in television."

Fowler was quick. "So you can be dropped from the will."

"And leave Natalie. But I'm not going, Mr. Fowler. Jack and Bates are fighting—literally. Jack beat Bates up but Bates is the stronger man, not physically, but he is hell-bent on running this show. I think Jack has honestly changed his mind. Whatever he intended in the first place, he now wants to continue his life with Natalie."

I looked out of the booth again. "I've got to hurry. Bates drove me to the shopping center but his wife came along. I think she's afraid of what Bates might do to me. I want to get back before I am missed."

"I won't keep you. I'll call at once to say I'm driving up to Alcott tonight and I'm going to have a long talk with Natalie. It may shatter her, but at least it will keep her alive. And before going I'll check on this man Grace. I wonder if her hiring him means that Natalie herself has had her suspicions about Clifford. If she has, it will intensify any danger she may be in. And I owe you an apology, Constance. An abject apology. I failed to see just how fine a woman you are. I hope Struthers can keep an eye on you until I get everything straightened out."

"I'm so glad you're coming, and I'll stay here as long as it is necessary."

"Yes," he said thoughtfully, "I think you'd better stay there, at least until after I've seen Natalie and made her see the light of day about her will. Oh, what's the name of that victim?"

For a moment I thought he meant the man who had been stabbed to death in Alcott and then I remembered. "You mean Gertrude Evans. She was a Boston woman. Now I must run."

I did. Bates, thank heavens, was not hovering outside the telephone booth, but he was outside the drugstore.

"Looked all over for you," he said eyeing suspiciously my package of pantyhose. "Freda still has lunch to get."

"Sorry. I had to wait for the druggist. He was busy with another customer and I wanted to know whether he could fill a prescription for me but, of course, he can't fill one from an out-of-town doctor."

Freda was standing at the corner, waiting. She was obviously taking no chance on Bates, though what he could conceivably do to me on the sidewalk with people passing was more than I could imagine.

I took my package up to my room, had a quick wash, powdered my nose, and applied some lipstick. When I went down to the drawing room, Tim rather ostentatiously glanced at his watch and Jack brought me a glass of sherry. Natalie, he said, would not join us for lunch. She'd have a tray in her room. The morning session had tired her. Tim looked up at him, looked down again.

"I should have told you, Constance," Jack said, "any time you have errands you can take the car." So he didn't like the idea of Bates driving me.

"Thank you, but I can't drive." I was tempted to say that

174

Freda had gone along for my protection, but I thought I'd leave any shocks to Mr. Fowler.

"Then please call on me. It would be doing me a favor, give me something to do beyond playing around in that workroom in the basement. I mean that." There was a look of strain on his handsome face, he smiled less often than he had in the beginning. He sipped sherry. "I'm worried about Natalie," he said abruptly. "She was doing so well, so miraculously well. Every day she could accomplish more and she didn't get tired. But something—" He made a vague gesture.

Tim took his usual leisurely time filling and lighting his pipe. "You think that working on the book is too much for her?"

"I'm afraid so. Not that I don't agree that it's a fine idea and you're the best man to do it, but at present—"

Neither Tim nor I spoke, letting him work it out for himself.

"Why," Jack asked abruptly, as though the idea had just occurred to him, "don't you two get married and go on your honeymoon? And then, later on, when Natalie is more like herself, you could take up the book project again."

"Nothing," Tim assured him, with a loving look at me that made me want to hit him, "would suit me better. But Mrs. Clifford has been so urgent about going on with it. She—" He looked at me for help.

"She begged me to stay," I said, "for a little while, so we could get better acquainted. I can't bear to walk out on her when she has been so wonderful, not only telling me to make this my permanent home but leaving half her estate to me—" I tossed the ball back to Tim. We might have been fellow conspirators for years the way we caught each other's signals.

"Well, my love, you can hardly go on living here after we're married. My work takes me all around and that's

175

where you are going too. You know: 'Whither thou goest.' Also I have to put in some time in Hollywood getting that pilot film set up. Another thing, Kate, you can hardly expect your aunt to divide her estate now that you're marrying a man of substance." He puffed out his chest and Jack laughed aloud. I thought Tim was overdoing it. There was no question that Jack wanted desperately to get me out of the house, but whether for my own safety or some other reason, I didn't know.

"Natalie certainly wouldn't want you to lose out on a fantastic deal like that, Struthers. Suppose we put it up to her that she really owed it to you to let you do your Hollywood stint now and come back to the book later."

Bates stood in the doorway, his hands at his sides. "Luncheon is served," he said, as though he was always the correct houseman, as though he hadn't cursed his wife, as though he hadn't said, "Some lousy actor," knowing who the man was who called himself Edwin Booth.

Jack stopped on the way to the table to answer the telephone. "Oh! . . . Why, yes, yes, of course. Natalie will be delighted. . . . Before dinner today? Fine. That is—there isn't anything wrong, is there? . . . Well, of course, I hoped it might be something you could put in a letter. Natalie is a bit worn-out and not up to coping with any serious problem." His voice trailed off. "Your room will be ready for you though Natalie might not be up to seeing you tonight. She's keeping to her own room today."

So Natalie hadn't told him about the threatening letters. He didn't know why she was in hiding.

Once during the afternoon I tapped lightly at Natalie's door and heard her quick "Who is it?"

"Constance."

"Oh, come in, dear. I wasn't sleeping. That is, I slept for a little while, but I dreamed of a knife and woke myself up whimpering. I've just been lying here."

"Natalie," I said abruptly, "why don't you get up and come downstairs? You're shutting yourself away as though—"

"As though I could run away from fate?"

"Oh, nonsense! Anyhow, you'll want to get up when Mr. Fowler comes."

"Brendon! Why is he coming?"

"I don't know. Jack talked to him, tried to persuade him to put it off or write to you. He said you were worn-out. He thinks Tim and I should get married right away and go to Hollywood while Tim works on that pilot film, and then, when you are ready, we could come back."

Natalie's hand clutched mine. It was burning hot. "But you aren't going, are you? You won't leave me?"

"Not until you want me to go," I promised rashly.

"Thank God for you," Natalie said. "You're sure about Timothy, aren't you? That is, sure that he really has a promising future?"

"I don't suppose there is anything sure in life," I said.

"But you're willing to take your chance?"

I nodded.

Natalie smiled at me but she did not agree to come down to dinner. In fact, when I left her room, I heard the click as she turned the key in the lock.

II

Natalie did not come down to dinner. She sent a warm message to Mr. Fowler saying she was looking forward to a long talk in the morning but explaining that she was too exhausted to join us that evening. Alice delivered the message with the air of a person accusing us, individually and collectively, of causing Natalie's exhaustion.

"I can't believe," the lawyer said when Alice had gone to speak to Freda in the kitchen, "that it is good for Natalie to have that woman around. Sometimes she acts hardly normal and Natalie needs healthy, cheerful, optimistic people around her." Unexpectedly he smiled at me, at least it was a pretty good attempt at a smile from a man who didn't seem to have much practice. "People like you," he said.

"Unfortunately," Jack put in, "at least, unfortunately for us, Struthers has a higher claim on Constance. He is going to marry her and carry her off to Hollywood."

"But not immediately," I put in before Tim could say anything.

Jack was making a terrific effort to be his usual pleasant, outgoing self, the agreeable host, but he was finding it heavy going. Tim wasn't helping beyond the elementary demands of good manners. So Brendon Fowler found himself cast in the unusual position of having to carry the conversational ball practically unaided.

When two or three gambits had failed, he startled us by saying, "I understand you've had a murder here in Alcott. Queer story, from all I can make out. No one seems to know whether the missing Edwin Booth is murderer or intended victim. That's a new twist to me." He turned to Tim. "Finding solutions to crimes that have never been cleared off the books is your specialty, isn't it?"

"Well, in a small way."

"I should think this one would be right up your alley."

Tim did not look at me. "I've got about all I can handle right now, sir, what with Mrs. Clifford's biography and this television pilot film coming up, and a possible series to follow."

"You mean the case hasn't interested you?" Fowler's surprised incredulity was a bit overdone and I looked at him quickly. "When you've had a private investigator right in the house here, too!"

Bates, carrying a platter of curried lamb, stopped short and his wheezing was the only sound in the room.

"Investigator?" Jack said, puzzled.

"This man Grace who's been working for Natalie."

"Oh," Jack said in a tone of relief, "he's a specialist on local history and the Netherfield family. He has a lot of material for Natalie. She was telling Struthers and me at lunch. Some awfully amusing stuff. Didn't you think so?"

Tim nodded, helping himself to rice, lamb and curry with a lavish hand. No matter what happened, nothing seemed to affect that man's appetite.

"Natalie told you the stories came from Grace?" Fowler tried to keep both Jack and Bates under observation. "But you didn't actually hear the stories from Grace himself?"

"No, I—" Jack put down his fork, stared at Fowler, half bewildered, half angry. "What are you getting at?"

"I'm trying to find out why Natalie thought it necessary to hire a private detective; why, if she had some problem, she didn't confide in me." Fowler added belatedly, "Or in you."

Eighteen

That night Jack drank four highballs after dinner. He wasn't staggering, but his voice was a trifle thick and his eyes glittered. Once he went up and tapped at Natalie's door but, after a low-toned colloquy, he came down again. He went into the kitchen and after a word with Freda went back to the garage apartment.

Having shot his bolt, Mr. Fowler seemed to be satisfied with the results and settled himself as usual in the library with his eternal chessboard.

"Everything's under control," Tim said in a low tone. "Let's get out of this mausoleum and taste the sinful delights of the village, a movie and hot chocolate at the drugstore, or, if you're feeling adventurous, a gin and tonic and some dancing at the Blue Boar. The music isn't too bad, no rock and roll. No one on dope, at least so far as I could make out."

"You seem to get around."

"I cased the joint to make sure it was suitable for my fiancée," he said virtuously.

As I hesitated, he added, "Nothing can happen to Natalie tonight, not with Fowler in the house. You can bet on that."

So, after Tim called to Jack and asked permission to use the car, we went to the Blue Boar, had gin and tonic, and danced a couple of times. Tim was an awful dancer and I'd had little practice, so we were evenly matched and we had fun. We had a lot of fun. I laughed more than I ever had before. And we never once referred to the problems besetting Natalie, or to the detective Grace, or the threatening letters, or even my father. We might not have had a single problem on our hands. In fact, we didn't have.

It was a little after twelve when we came home. The house, including the library, was dark. For a moment Tim held me close in his arms and kissed me, gentle, loving kisses, but he whispered suddenly, "God, I wish we could have been married today!" Then he released me and we went quietly upstairs with Alice trudging almost on our heels.

"Waiting for you," she said. "You need your rest. I brought you a nice glass of hot milk."

I was more surprised than grateful at any attention from that quarter, but I said, "Thank you. That's very thoughtful, Alice."

She nodded and then waited, her arms folded, for Tim to go into his own room. Over her head he looked at the milk and shook his head slightly.

I closed the door of my room, smelled the milk, and took a tiny sip, barely moistening my lips. It had a bitter taste. I was about to empty the glass and then, feeling rather foolish and melodramatic, I hid it in my clothes closet, which, I thought, was what Tim wanted; not that I could be in any real danger from Alice.

I put the matter out of my mind, locked my door as usual, opened the window a trifle and went to bed. I lay thinking not of the milk to which something unpleasant had been added, but of Tim, his gaiety, his gentle kisses, and the controlled passion with which he had wished this were our wedding night. That night I didn't even dream. I was so happy I slept deeply and restfully, so deeply that I was unaware of the usual morning sounds in the house, the swish with which the draperies were drawn back in the drawing room and library, the bustle in the kitchen, Tim banging around his room like an enraged bumblebee while he dressed.

Sunlight in my eyes awakened me. Then I heard Alice saying, "You needn't bother with Mrs. Clifford's tray. I'll take it in. And don't call Miss Armstrong. She was up till all hours and she'll probably sleep late. Girls that age! And no one knowing what they may be up to. If I hadn't let them see I was keeping an eye on them, I'd hate to think what would have happened. No morals."

I swung my legs off the bed. Evidently dancing was just what the lame one had needed. It felt fine. This morning I could even risk a shower without fear of falling.

I had just slipped my feet into bedroom slippers and I was reaching for the taffeta robe when I heard the screaming. It went on and on, like a whistling teakettle magnified a hundred times.

Natalie, I thought. Oh, God, Natalie!

Three doors were flung open at one time as Tim, Mr. Fowler, and I burst out into the hall. The maid was running up the stairs white-faced. Then, to my indescribable relief, I heard Natalie cry out in terror, "What is it? What is it?"

Alice opened the door of Jack's room and plunged out into the hall. Her neat white apron, which she always insisted on wearing over a trim black dress, was stained with blood. Her mouth opened and closed and then she fell on the floor—fell headlong like a log.

"Look after her, will you?" Tim called to the maid, stepped over the prone body, and went into Jack's room. The wait seemed interminable until he came out, his face unrevealing.

Mr. Fowler and I spoke together. "What is it?"

182

Tim looked down at Alice. "She's just fainted. She'll be all right."

"What is it?" the maid asked. "Shall I get a doctor?"

"Yes, you'd better get a doctor for Mrs. Clifford."

"But Mr.—"

"Mr. Clifford won't need a doctor. He is dead. You'd better call the police. The man has been murdered. Stabbed to death."

The lawyer brushed past him and went into Jack's room. When he came out, his face was colorless but he was in full command. "I'll call the police. Struthers, I want you to get hold of Bates and don't let him go. Understand?"

Tim nodded and ran down the stairs. I heard him make some hasty reply to Freda's frightened question and then the back door slammed as he ran out toward the garage apartment.

Mr. Fowler turned to me. "You'd better go to Natalie. It's a tough job for you, but you're the only one who can handle it. I'm relying on you to keep your head and, if you can, help her to keep hers. She can't afford another breakdown."

"This will kill her," I said, or thought I said, but no words came out.

I think the hardest thing I ever did in my life was opening Natalie's door. I took a long breath and went in. She wasn't there, but the doors of the bathroom shared by the two bedrooms were both wide open and Natalie was in Jack's room, standing beside his bed, looking down.

I had to go and take her by the arm, turn her away from the man who lay as though asleep except for the blood-stained bedding. There was no sign of a struggle, his head was turned to the wall as though he had been asleep.

I almost dragged Natalie, unresisting but not helping, as though she moved automatically, into her sitting room and settled her on the chaise longue. The great somber eyes looked at me without appearing to see me. Somehow the beauty had drained out of her, leaving her almost old, almost ugly.

Her lips moved and I thought she was trying to speak and I bent over her. "The knife," she said. "That man warned me about a knife."

I started to shake her, to arouse her, but it was kinder to leave her in this state of numbness. The pain would begin soon enough. Too soon.

She said only one thing more: "The four-leaf clover. I told you it was the gift of life and the gift of death."

She did not speak again. She lay back on the long chair, apparently relaxed, but her eyes were open, huge and blank, looking at nothing, looking at an empty future, looking at the end of happiness.

I turned to see Freda in the doorway. She held a tray with two cups of coffee. Her face was ghastly but her hands were steady.

"How like you to think of this!" I exclaimed.

She forced a smile. "I guess I'm more a nurse than anything else, after all," she said.

I lifted a cup and held it to Natalie's lips. "Try to drink a little."

She obeyed like a nicely brought up small child, sip by sip, until the cup was half empty and then she waved it away with an impatient gesture.

"You'd better drink yours," Freda said to me.

"How about you?"

"I've got to get breakfast for them all: Mr. Fowler and Mr. Struthers and probably the police."

"The police are here already?"

"Just drove up." She went to close the bathroom doors, but Natalie did not notice. She did not notice when men tramped up the stairs, paused briefly as they caught sight of Jack's quiet body and the bloodstained bedding, and then went in. I had expected loud voices and trampling, but these men were quiet.

"I hope the doctor hurries," Freda said.

"How about Alice?"

Freda shrugged. "She's all right. Just plain wild because Mr. Fowler sent you in instead of her, though she was out as flat as a dead mackerel at the time. I think she's half out of her mind. She kept saying, 'She shouldn't be here! She shouldn't have waked up.' She's down in the kitchen now. No, we'll need the doctor for Mrs. Clifford. I don't like her color and that's a fact." She put her fingers on Natalie's pulse and her lips tightened. "We'll have two bodies if we aren't careful."

I meant to stop her, but it didn't matter. Natalie didn't hear. She didn't speak again, but when I started to get up from where I crouched beside her chair, she clutched at my hand. There were things to be done and I wanted to get dressed but I gave up the idea. For the time being it was more important to give Natalie the reassurance of my presence.

Freda went down to the kitchen and I heard Bates cursing as he struggled with Tim. "Let me go, damn you! I haven't done anything. If anyone killed Jack, it wasn't me. I wanted him alive. You may not believe that but I wanted him alive. He's no good to me dead. Let me go!"

"Don't carry on so, Joe," Freda said. "Here, drink some coffee. No one can blame you for what happened to the man. You were with me all night. I can swear to that. All night."

Alice's voice rose shrilly. "You don't have to look far! It's that niece. I knew she was trouble from the beginning. Like her mother. Tried to make up to Mr. Clifford. And then wanted him out of the way so she and her boy friend could get all Mrs. Clifford's estate. Only I don't see how she woke

up. She shouldn't have woke up." Alice was almost screaming. There was the sound of a sharp clap and I realized that
Freda had slapped her. The hysteria stopped and Alice
began to sob.

I closed the door to shut out the sounds, but it didn't
matter. Natalie had withdrawn so far I could not reach her
at all. Only that feverish clutch on my hand indicated that
she knew I was there. Something in her seemed to shrivel
and die before my eyes. There was no thought behind the
great dark eyes, no color in her face, no expression around
the lax mouth. This, I thought, is how I'll look not at forty
or sixty but perhaps at eighty. Whoever had plunged that
knife into Jack might as well have murdered his wife too.

More police had come now and Fowler was herding
some of them down to the library to talk. At the same time
the doctor arrived and the police called him into Jack's
room. He was there barely ten minutes. As he came out I
heard him say, "Sometime around midnight, might be two
o'clock at the latest. The first stab killed him. The second
slid off a bone. The others—two? no, three—were made
after he was dead."

"What about the weapon? He took it with him."

"A sharp point, a blade about six inches long, I'd say—
I can tell better when I've opened him up. God! Why did
I ever take the job of coroner? Three-edged blade, just like
the one that killed the poor devil at the rooming house."

"My God!" one of the policemen exclaimed. "What have
we got here, a homicidal maniac?"

"That's your job, thank God! Now I'd better see Mrs.
Clifford."

"We'll have to talk to her."

"Not now you don't. Maybe later this afternoon. Maybe
tomorrow. I know her constitution." He opened the door
and came in. He stood looking down at Natalie, his face
grim, his fingers on her pulse.

"Mrs. Clifford," he said gently. There was a shadowy figure in the doorway and I saw the uniform of a state trooper. "Mrs. Clifford," the doctor said more loudly. The blank eyes did not even glance in his direction, there was no response.

"Get hold of that woman who trained as a nurse," the doctor told me. "Mrs. Clifford is in deep shock. I'll want a heating pad and some extra blankets, and get her into bed at once."

"I think Freda is cooking breakfast."

"Well, cook it yourself, girl! This is an emergency." He snorted. "Breakfast!"

The trooper moved out of the doorway and went downstairs without a word while I went to the kitchen where Bates was digging into a mound of what looked like about six scrambled eggs, and making disgusting gobbling sounds. Tim, standing beside his chair, was drinking coffee and watching his prisoner.

I explained to Freda what the doctor wanted. "Maybe the maid can finish up," she said. "The grapefruit is ready to serve and there are muffins in the oven and some fried ham nearly done. I guess she can scramble the eggs. I've been teaching her because she is planning to get married."

She took a last look at Joe and then went quickly up the stairs. Freda was quite a woman.

Alice, who had been staring at me as though I were a specter, pushed aside her untasted breakfast and went out of the kitchen. I heard a trooper stop her as she started up the stairs.

"Where do you think you're going?"

"I'm Mrs. Clifford's personal maid. She needs me."

"She doesn't need you now. She's got a nurse with her. Doctor's orders." He silenced Alice's shrill protest. "Just keep out of the way, will you? We've got things to do."

The rest of the morning passed in a kind of orderly

confusion. The maid took over the kitchen with unexpected competence. Freda must be an efficient teacher. In fact, she had been good at everything but choosing a husband.

"I'll take coffee into the little dining room for the police," the maid said. "If the rest of you could eat out here, it would be a big help."

It didn't seem possible that I could eat but I did, and Tim tackled his plate with his usual enthusiasm, though he didn't take his eyes off Bates who, once he had finished eating, sat sullen, deflated, and frightened. His overweight body seemed to have collapsed like a balloon, the fat folding in on him in an obscene sort of way. Now and then he wheezed.

Once Tim asked, "How is Natalie?"

I shook my head. "It's awful. She just lies there staring at nothing. Thank heaven for Freda. She's a tower of strength."

Mr. Fowler came into the kitchen, accompanied by a couple of troopers, and Tim stood up. "He's all yours," he said cheerfully, hauling Bates out of his chair.

"I didn't do it," Bates whined. "I didn't. I swear it. Ask my wife. I want a lawyer. I got a right to a lawyer."

"You're sure going to need one," the younger of the troopers said.

At the low-toned order of an older man in plain clothes the young trooper went out to the garage apartment, to search, I supposed, for the weapon with which Jack had been stabbed.

Mr. Fowler took Bates's chair, after a distasteful look at the mess he had made of things, and the maid came to wipe off the table and bring him a plate of ham and eggs and flaky muffins. She poured coffee and told the troopers she had made an extra pot of coffee and left it with cups and saucers, cream and sugar, at the small end of the dining room.

188

"Take him down to the station house," the senior man said, "and book him as a material witness." Bates, still howling for a lawyer, was led away. It was only when he had gone that I had my first doubt.

"Mr. Fowler, there's no reason I can see why Bates would kill Jack. They were business partners in a way. Bates couldn't do a thing without Jack. They might disagree, they might fight, but they sort of had to stand together."

"And if it wasn't Bates?" Fowler asked at his driest. When I made no reply, he prodded me. "Well?"

I had been busy assimilating a new idea. "There's only one person who would really want Jack dead. That's Alice. She has always hated him because he came first with Natalie. You remember her stories about those two attempts to murder her on her honeymoon?" The detective from the state police stiffened to attention.

"Suppose she made it all up? You've said yourself she is hysterical and a bad influence on Natalie. She could easily have written those anonymous warning letters and left them in Natalie's room. She has done everything she could to drive me away. She hated my mother. She hates me. Last night—wait, I'll show you." I got up from the table.

"Where are you going?" the detective asked.

"Up to my room. There's something—"

"Not now," he said. "Not yet." Then I heard it, the shuffling feet of men carrying a heavy burden down the stairs and the slam of a door as an ambulance took Jack away from his home.

"All right," the detective said then, "I'll go with you."

I led the way up the stairs. There were still a couple of troopers in Jack's room. The door stood open, the bloodstained bedding thrown back. The door to Natalie's room opened and the doctor came out, closing it quietly behind him.

"How is she?" I whispered.

He shook his head.

"I suppose," the detective said cynically, "you gave her something to make her sleep."

"No, I tried a stimulant. There's not much I can do. She's in deep shock. She should be in a hospital with round-the-clock nursing, if there is such a thing to be found, but the only response I got from her was when I suggested it. She acted frantic. Thank God for Mrs. Bates. Sensible as they come and calm. Now where is that damned-fool Alice? I understand she fainted and then threw a fit of hysterics. I'd better take a look at her."

"Don't give her a sedative or anything like that just now, Doctor," I said.

"Why not?"

"Because I don't think the police have the right person. I think Alice—" I led the way to my room, told them quickly about Alice and the unaccustomed glass of hot milk, and Tim's warning shake of the head. And how, this morning, she had screamed that I shouldn't be here, I should never have waked up. I reached for the glass and the detective practically yelped at me. Then he picked it up with what looked like a large pair of tongs, slid a plastic cover over it, working deftly, and handed it to the doctor.

"Better check on this, just in case—"

"I'd like to get dressed," I said, and the detective nodded, went through my room with a fine-tooth comb, looking, I assumed, for the knife, and then let me go in. He followed the doctor up the stairs to the attic room occupied by Alice.

When I came down, I found Fowler and Tim in the library, each with what looked to me like a hefty slug of whisky before him. As I raised my brows, Tim said, "Leave us not be censorious. We needed this. So do you." And he brought me a glass of sherry.

It wasn't until I had dropped into one of the deep leather

chairs that I realized how much I needed it. My mind hadn't yet come to terms with the astounding fact that it was not Natalie but Jack who had been murdered.

"How's Natalie?" Fowler asked at length, breaking a long silence.

"In shock. The doctor wanted her in a hospital, but she resisted, so he gave it up. Fortunately Freda trained as a nurse."

"And her husband may be a murderer."

"What about that milk?" Tim asked.

"I took a tiny sip and it tasted bitter. I hid the glass and the trooper gave it to the doctor to analyze."

"Looks to me as though we had all landed in a madhouse," Tim commented.

"A nest of vipers," I agreed, "with Alice in the role of head viper."

"No," Fowler said, "there is something we have missed. We and the police. Apparently Clifford was stabbed with the same weapon that killed the poor devil in the rooming house. The doctor isn't sure, but it seems to be a fair chance. After all, two killers, using practically identical weapons and identical methods, killing their victim while he slept, are a shade unlikely, at least in a village of this size. And, damn it, Alice could not have been out in that violent storm."

"Actually," Tim pointed out, "any one of us could have been out in it, unknown to the others. Any one of us."

"What we need," Fowler said, "is to find that man Grace. Why did Natalie hire a private detective without consulting me? What in hell could he do for her that would be worth twenty-five thousand dollars?"

I didn't look at Tim. I was remembering that Grace had known about my father and had followed him to Alcott. For the first time I was afraid.

Nineteen

All that day the police came and went, but there were no personal calls. News travels fast in a village and neighbors had seen the police, the doctor and the ambulance with the covered stretcher that had been carried out. Freda remained with Natalie, conscientious, efficient, watching her pulse and her blood pressure, but her eyes were almost as blank as Natalie's.

All we knew about Bates was that he had been booked as a material witness and had been allowed to make one telephone call. The man he called was a Boston lawyer who apparently referred him to a local man. Boston again. The police were checking with Boston to find out what they could about Bates and any previous record. And on one John Clifford, now deceased.

The doctor had eventually and mercifully stopped Alice's wild screaming and got her in a condition in which she was able to answer the trooper's questions. Then, with the trooper's consent and probably to his relief, the doctor gave her a shot to put her to sleep.

The doctor stopped at Natalie's room. When he came out, he was still grave. "She ought to be in a hospital, but she refuses to leave the house. It's the only response I can get out of her. Anyhow, we haven't a large enough nursing staff and she needs more than the occasional look-in of an overworked floor nurse. Mrs. Bates is being fine, but she can't keep it up without relief. I suggest, Miss Armstrong, that you take over about five o'clock while she prepares the dinner. Then she can sleep until midnight when she'll relieve you. Would that be satisfactory?"

I nodded. "If you'll tell me what to do."

"Just be there. If there is any change, call me, no matter what time it is."

"What sort of change?"

The doctor shrugged. "She may come out of this daze and go into hysterics. She may get overexcited. She has a long history of nervous ailments and years of invalidism." He patted my shoulder. "You're too young for all this, and it has been a day of bad shocks with a murder in the house."

"And a murderer," Tim said. "One thing sure, I stay on guard all night."

"A nice heroic gesture," Fowler said tartly, "but with Bates behind bars and Alice under sedation, I can hardly see what purpose you will serve."

The doctor looked from one man to the other but he was accustomed to unreasonable tensions in a case where the members of a household have sustained a profound shock and he went out, carrying his black bag and a small plastic bag containing the glass of milk Alice had given me.

I suppose there wasn't a possibility, however foolish, however nonsensical, that the three of us didn't discuss that day.

Once Fowler said, "You know I wonder whether it is possible that a mistake was made last night and the wrong person killed. Unless Alice is off her rocker, I can't see any reason for someone killing Clifford. Everything, including the letters, points to Natalie as the intended victim."

"Everything?" Tim asked. "They must obviously have been Alice's work designed to make Natalie distrust Clifford and Kate, a kind of lust to destroy anything that comes between her and the object of her devotion. A single-minded sense of possession. You find it in cannibal mothers. It scares hell out of me."

The telephone rang and I went to answer it. The editor of the Alcott *Reporter* said rather apologetically that there were widespread rumors of trouble at the house. I told him —there was no use holding back the story—that Mr. Clifford had been murdered and the houseman was in the custody of the police. He must understand that, at this time, it would be impossible for him to talk to any member of the family.

The news must have been on radio and television within an hour because of Natalie's fame, but, though men with press cards in their hats began to appear in every kind of car, no one rang the bell and Fowler got on the phone and asked the police to keep them away.

Sometime early in the afternoon the maid set plates of sandwiches and a pot of coffee on the small table. Later the doctor telephoned and talked first to Fowler and then to the trooper who had remained in the house. When Fowler came back, he paused for a moment and put his hand on my shoulder.

"That milk," he said, and his voice was husky with shock, "contained at least six of Natalie's powerful painkillers. It looks as though Alice tried to kill you. They are asking Freda to go up with the trooper, rouse Alice, and get her dressed."

"Is she being taken to the police station?"

"No, the hospital. She must be mad. God, when I think of that woman being around Natalie, it's a wonder to me it didn't drive her straight over the brink."

Tim came to lift me out of my chair and sit down with me on his lap. "Oh, God," he whispered. "Suppose you had drunk that milk. Suppose you had!"

And then Freda came down the stairs. "Miss Armstrong, will you stay with Mrs. Clifford while I see what can be

194

done for Alice?" Instead of drawn fatigue, as I would have expected, she looked relaxed and relieved, and I realized she was aware that Alice's attempt at murder would help Bates. There could hardly be two killers in the house. "I guess that lets Joe out."

"You don't think so, do you?" Tim asked Fowler when Freda had gone up to Alice.

"I think Alice tried to kill Constance because of jealousy. I would be almost certain she killed Clifford for the same reason, but—"

"Well?" Tim prodded him.

"There's the man in the rooming house and the same weapon that killed Clifford. I wish to God the police could lay hands on the man who called himself Edwin Booth."

That was when the telephone rang again and this time the lawyer took the call. I heard him give a startled exclamation. There was a long pause and then he said, for once shaken out of his calm, "Good God! . . . It would not be permitted at this time . . . I suppose you realize . . . You don't know what you are doing . . ." He came back into the drawing room where Tim and I waited, staring at him.

He wiped his head. "Constance," he said abruptly, "that was your father. He's just heard the news. First he wanted you out of the house. Then, when I said you couldn't leave now, he said he was on his way here."

"Oh, no!" I cried. "Oh, no!"

Fowler's eyes were intent and cold. "So you knew all the time that he was Edwin Booth."

"Yes, I knew. But he might as well jump into a lion's den as come here and identify himself. Who is going to believe that he is innocent?"

"I believe it," Tim said. "I can guarantee one thing, Fowler. No stranger entered this house last night, unless he was Houdini. I checked every lock before I went to bed and I slept with my door open and never closed it until I

195

got up to dress this morning."

"And you're in love with the man's daughter," Fowler said. "Who will trust your judgment?"

"But why would my father stab to death a man he'd never seen, never heard of?"

Fowler shrugged. "You'd better get up to Natalie, and don't tell her about your father. She has enough to bear."

And once more an ambulance drove up to the house and a stretcher was carried in. A few minutes later it came back with Alice, apparently sleeping.

As I went up the stairs, I heard the telephone ring again.

II

Natalie was lying in bed but she had thrown out the heating pad and pushed away the down comforter. She was flushed and when I took her pulse, as I had learned to do with my mother, it was racing, and her hand was dry and burning hot. She had a high fever.

I signaled to Tim, who was standing at the top of the stairs, and shaped the words "Fever . . . doctor." He nodded and went back to the telephone where Fowler was still talking. Then, before Tim could use the phone, Fowler had called the trooper and had him listen to the call.

Natalie's eyes were glittering and her lips were parched. I poured cold water and lifted her head while she drank thirstily. She muttered something. It sounded like, "Put out the light," but the light was not burning.

"What's—happening?" she asked with difficulty.

I didn't know how to answer. I said cautiously, "Do you remember—?"

"Jack. Yes. Oh, yes!" A long shudder shook her body. "Is he—?"

"No, he isn't here," I said gently.

"And he won't be. Never again. Never, never again."

There was no adequate answer I could make. Natalie was too intelligent to lie to. She would never have accepted any easy platitudes about God moving in a mysterious way or that he had died quite peacefully and painlessly. He had not known death was coming. Instead, I found myself thinking of Prince Hal's comment to Falstaff: "Thou owest God a death."

After a few minutes Natalie asked fretfully, "Where is Alice? It isn't like her not to be here when I need her."

I thought fast. Natalie had had enough shocks. "She was so upset about Jack's death, knowing what it would do to you, that she went into a sort of collapse and the doctor thought it wise to take her to the hospital. She was hysterical and he was afraid she would upset the whole household."

"So she has gone too." Natalie turned her head away. "Sooner or later, everyone leaves me: Florence ran away with George; my mother died; my father died; for years I might as well have been dead. Then there was Jack. The impossible dream of happiness. The wonderful hope for an invalid that restored her to life. The miracle. Do you believe in miracles, Constance? A miracle so bright, so blinding—so blinding—" A long pause.

"He has left me. And now Alice. They have all gone. Except you. But you'll stay, won't you? You won't go away. You'll have everything now, you know, when I die. If you want the capital, it's quite a lot because I never spent a third of my income and the money mounted up. And I have a lot of bonds in a safety deposit box I never told anyone about. And there's this house. Stay with me and you'll be a rich woman someday."

Her grip on my hand tightened until it hurt me. Bargaining with God, I thought, with a surge of pity.

And then the doorbell rang. "I can't see anyone," she said feverishly.

"You won't have to."

Downstairs I could hear the doctor's voice. He was talking to Tim and Mr. Fowler. The trooper was still carrying on that long telephone conversation.

Before the doctor could come up the stairs, the trooper said, "Doctor, just a minute, please."

I got up to close the door and Natalie's hand reached for mine. "I'm not leaving you," I assured her. "I was just going to shut the door."

"Shut the door," she repeated. "I mustn't do that again, Constance. Shut out life. I mustn't do that."

"Perhaps," I suggested, "you would like to travel."

"No, I've just got back from a long, long journey. I'm going to write a poem, Constance. The best poem I've ever written. It will be a long poem; I can feel it shaping in my mind, not the words but the feelings. I'm going to call it 'Requiem for a Lost Love.' "

There was a tap at the door and the doctor came in. He looked at Natalie, thrust a thermometer into her mouth and took her pulse. Then he said, his voice grave, "I think we'll have to put you in the hospital for a while."

"No, Doctor, no!"

"I'm afraid so, Mrs. Clifford. It's—the best way."

She looked at him then, her eyes widening. He returned the look steadily and there was a vast pity in his face. Then she said, "Give me five minutes alone, will you? There's been so much to face today."

He hesitated, though the request seemed reasonable to me. Then he went into her bathroom and returned with a small bottle which he slipped into his pocket.

Unexpectedly her lovely smile transformed her face. "My painkiller! No, Doctor, I didn't expect it to kill that kind of pain." She smiled at me. "Go with him, will you, dear? I need a few minutes—quite alone—in which to find myself. I'm used to working out my problems alone."

So I preceded the doctor out of the room and he closed the door behind him. We went downstairs in silence and found Tim, Fowler, and the trooper in the drawing room, staring into the blazing fire that Tim had laid. The men weren't talking. Fowler looked stunned. Tim glanced quickly from the doctor to me.

"All right?"

"How could it be?" the doctor said.

"You're not—you didn't—"

"She wanted five minutes alone," the doctor said. "No, I didn't. It wasn't necessary. Anyhow," and he pulled the small bottle out of his pocket, "I brought this away with me."

"Is that what Alice used?" Tim asked.

"It's what was in Miss Armstrong's glass of milk, yes."

The doctor accepted a drink almost eagerly, but still no one seemed inclined to talk. They just waited.

It was Tim who said at last, "Look here, Kate's father will arrive before long. I think it is only fair that she should be put in the picture." He came to sit on the arm of my chair, holding me against him so my head rested on his shoulder.

"Don't make me wait," I said. "Anything is better than waiting."

"Put the child out of her agony," Fowler said. And then he went on himself, "You don't need to worry about your father, my dear. He didn't kill anyone. He came here only to see you and that's why he is on his way here now. After he heard of Clifford's murder—"

He stopped as though he expected me to understand what he was saying. I didn't.

Tim simply held me closer but he didn't attempt to speak. He seemed to be listening, almost as though this conversation did not concern him, did not interest him. Just listening.

The doctor stole a glance at his watch and took another hefty gulp of his drink.

It was the trooper who said, "Mrs. Clifford's lucky piece has been found. It was in the possession of a man named Grace. Private dick. Kicked off the New York force years ago for blackmail. Long before Watergate he might have been the inventor of dirty tricks."

I looked at him blankly. "But I don't see—"

The doctor glanced at his watch again, finished his drink in a series of long swallows, and set down the glass with an air of finality. Tim did not move, still listening. Then the doctor went heavily up the stairs and opened Natalie's door.

III

She was still living, blood spurting through her fingers, which clutched the handle of the stiletto letter opener in her hand, the great jewel sparkling in the light. She looked at the doctor and her smile was almost mischievous. "I had it hidden under the mattress."

I clutched the doctor's arm. "Aren't you going to do anything?"

"There's nothing to do."

"Thank you, Doctor." Natalie's voice was weaker. "It was kind of you, giving me my five minutes."

He nodded without speaking. A long rattling breath almost shook her body and she was gone. There was nothing of Natalie. Just a quiet, still body, the small hand still tightly clutched around the knife handle and all the beauty, all the poetry, had gone.

I knelt beside her, sobbing. "We shouldn't have left her. We should never have left her. Knowing her grief—"

The doctor drew me to my feet. "Mercy or justice? Sometimes you have to make a hard decision."

"Justice?" I protested as he led me firmly to the door and called for Freda.

"Oh, yes. I think we will find that is the knife that killed her husband and the poor fellow in the rooming house. A murderer twice over, God help her! And nearly three times. She's the one who fixed that drink for you, Miss Armstrong, and instructed Alice to give it to you. Alice told me when she woke up in the ambulance. She knew the thing had gone too far and had to be stopped. That's why she wrote the letters. You see she saw Mrs. Clifford come home the night of the storm, and found her soaked clothes the next day. Poor Alice did her best to protect Mrs. Clifford."

Twenty

The doctor came to take my pulse and suggest a sedative. I shook my head. "There is nothing wrong with me. I'm just—dazed, I guess. I don't understand anything."

"Wait until Grace gets here," Fowler said.

"But why Grace and how did he get hold of Natalie's lucky piece?" I asked.

Fowler leaned back in his chair. His skin was gray and I saw the fine lines in it as though he had aged during the day. I remembered that he had loved Natalie, loved her perhaps more than anyone had except Alice, whose devotion was obsessive, stifling.

Freda brought me a cup of coffee and a piece of gingerbread. "You'll need something. Dinner is going to be late."

"Dinner!"

"People have to eat, no matter what happens."

There was a loud-voiced colloquy outside the house and then the trooper stationed inside took part and came back to say, "There's a man named George Armstrong out there who insists on coming in. He said if I gave you his name—"

I set down the tray Freda had brought me and shot out of the room. And there, after so long, stood my father. I flung myself into his arms and clung to him, sobbing into his shoulder. He held me without speaking but he bent his head so that his cheek rested on my hair. And at last I really looked at him. He had changed a lot. He looked as though he had been ill, his hair was almost white, he wore glasses, but his good looks were so bred in the bone that he was still handsome, distinguished enough to attract attention, as he always had, and his voice was still beautiful.

"Constance!" He held me off, looking at me. "How like Natalie you are! She won't like that. She won't like that at all. Natalie can't accept competition. Such a pity, too, because she has so much. Her trouble has always been that she wants everything." He shook his head. "I shouldn't say that in her house. Anyhow, it is a long time since I have felt any bitterness toward her. She is what she is."

"Father—Natalie's dead."

"She—what!"

"Just now. It's really horrible."

"I did her an injustice. I thought that illness of hers was purely self-imposed, an unconscious demand for sympathy and attention. I didn't realize it was serious."

"She killed herself, Father. Stabbed herself."

"Good God!"

I took him into the drawing room. "Mr. Fowler, this is my father."

My father nodded without offering his hand, but after a moment Fowler extended his own. "It's a long time, Armstrong."

"A long time," my father agreed.

"And this is Tim."

This time the handclasp was warm. "We have already become friends. And we'd better be." My father smiled then, the smile I remembered, the one that had captured so many hearts, and I realized: Why, he's not old at all. Just middle-aged. The prime of life. He can't be more than forty-five. If it weren't for the white hair and the weariness, which is a matter of mind rather than of body, he'd still be the George Armstrong of a few years ago.

"We will be friends, I hope," Tim said. "It won't be my fault if we aren't."

"I understand," Father said to me, "you are going to marry him."

"Well, he's never come right out and asked me," I said bitterly. "He just sort of edges around it."

And unexpectedly, all the men were laughing, even Mr. Fowler.

"If you think," Tim said, instantly taking advantage of the situation, "you are going to trick me into making a public proposal by these tactics, wench, you are wrong."

The telephone rang, the trooper answered it, and called Mr. Fowler.

The maid came in. "Mrs. Bates wants to know, sir, if you'd like some coffee and a sandwich. Dinner is going to be late tonight."

"Thank you. I had lunch at the terminal in New York."

"What the man needs is a drink," Tim said thoughtlessly.

My father shook his head "I don't drink. But coffee—that would be fine."

And then for the third time that day an ambulance drew up at the house and the same young attendants came in with a stretcher and, for the first time in my life, I went into hysterics.

"It's like *The Duchess of Malfi*; just corpses! Just bodies all over the place."

Tim slapped me hard across the cheek and I stopped, took a couple of long sobbing breaths, and most unhelpfully burst into tears. That made twice in a quarter of an hour.

"You'll probably cry at your own wedding," Tim said in a tone of disgust, but he had a steadying arm around me.

"What wedding?" I sniffed and groped for a handkerchief.

"Okay, you win," he said in a tone of resignation. "Lady,

will you marry me?"

"I'll take the matter into consideration."

"You," he said, shaking me, "will give me a flat yes or no right now." And then he kissed me. The warmth of his kiss and the comfort of his arms were still with me when the men came down the stairs again with their covered stretcher.

"May I?" Fowler looked from the doctor to the trooper. "May I see her once more?"

Silently the doctor drew back the sheet that covered her face. She was still beautiful, but the great eyes were closed and her lashes seemed to make shadows on the white cheeks. Her lips were slightly parted.

"How beautiful she was," Fowler said, almost in a whisper.

"As though," my father said, "she would catch another Antony in her strong toil of grace."

Gently the doctor covered her face again and Natalie was taken out of the house.

II

It must have been an hour later that Bates reappeared, driven by the police. He gave us a look half sheepish, half challenging, and went back to the kitchen where I heard Freda exclaim in relief, "Oh, thank heaven! But there's one thing, Joe. This is the last time you get involved in anything shady. Next time I leave you. Is that clear?"

"Whatever you say, sweetheart," Bates answered with a humility that I profoundly distrusted.

All the talk was desultory. The trooper inside had withdrawn, but he was needed to help the outside man keep the curious public moving on. In spite of the cold, the deepening twilight, and the fact that the house was dark, for all the draperies in the drawing room and library had been drawn to frustrate the curious, people kept gathering. The presence of the police, the arrival of three ambulances, had aroused curiosity to fever pitch.

Fowler was determined that nothing should be explained until the arrival of Grace, and he was clearly calling the turns.

Once my father ventured to say, "I take it I'm not under suspicion for the murder of that poor devil in the rooming house."

"Small credit to you," Fowler snapped. "Calling yourself Edwin Booth. Of all the damned fool things to do."

"It was indeed," my father agreed.

Fowler's brooding silence made us all uncomfortable. My father eased the situation by talking to Tim about his work; not Natalie's biography, of course, but his probable future in Hollywood.

Grateful to have a safe subject, Tim told him about the books he had written on unsolved murders. They had grown out of his work as a reporter and his following a case that had got nowhere. He had tried to work out what had happened and that started him on his books. Now he was to prepare a pilot film. If it was successful, there would probably be a series, using the cases from his books and possibly having him go into other cases.

"Not a nightly show, or even a weekly one, but a big special deal once a month, something with prestige. What's needed, of course, is not only a good script but a good cast, and not so much a good cast as one major star big enough to pull the series out of the crime-picture level. Someone like you, sir. With a name like George Armstrong heading the cast—"

My father sat staring at him. He took off his glasses and polished them. His mouth opened and closed. His hands were shaking. But when he spoke, his beautiful voice was under control.

"My dear boy, you must not let your love for this girl of mine distort your judgment. I've been hounded out of the studios. There's not one that would give me a job sweeping out the place."

"Have you ever wondered why?" Tim asked.

And the answer arrived five minutes later in the shape of Grace, former policeman, then blackmailer, then private investigator. Grace told his story calmly enough. It was all part of the day's work for him. He thought in terms of jobs and not of the people whose lives were affected. He had a ferret-like intelligence but no imagination. The thing called empathy had been left out of his makeup. Even while he described how he had wrecked Father's career, he could look him in the face, simply reporting a job well done.

"But," he said, "when it comes to murder, I want out. I'm not a violent man. After all, there's no sense in violence when you can handle things peacefully."

It wasn't a nice story. Natalie Netherfield had got in touch with him twenty years earlier after her sister had eloped with George Armstrong, one of America's most popular actors. She had been in love with George and had assumed, when he came so frequently to the house, that she was his object. When, instead, he married her sister she was frantic.

"So that was it," my father said. "So that was it! I never looked at anyone but Florence. I'd seen hundreds of glamour girls in Hollywood, but she was different. She was lovely and sweet. She was all I wanted. Her mother was like her in many ways and she saw how things were going between us and I think she approved. She felt that her husband had spoiled Natalie at Florence's expense. Anyhow, it was clear after I brought her home one night and he saw me kissing her good night that Mr. Netherfield was going to prevent our marriage if he could. He thought I belonged by divine right to Natalie. So we ran away."

Grace took up the story. He worked out of New York but he had an arrangement with a woman in a Los Angeles detective agency and they pooled their resources. Jane Turner, her name was. She was to keep an eye on Armstrong, find out where he was, how he lived, and smash his career if she could.

My father took a long breath and sat staring numbly at the havoc Natalie had created. Fowler covered his eyes with his hand, and did not move. Only Tim was bright-eyed and alert, nodding as though that was the way he had figured it out.

"You saw it, did you?" Grace asked.

"Well, I heard Mrs. Clifford's faithful and fanatical maid Alice speak to Mr. Fowler with such hatred of Florence that I began to wonder."

Ours, as I have said, had been a quiet, domestic home life, untypical of the Hollywood of two decades ago. And Jane began to plant her rumors, the sort of thing one woman tells another in a carrying voice in a restaurant like The Brown Derby, or hints to scandalmongers and the ubiquitous gossip columnists that infest Hollywood.

Her line, explained Grace coolly, was that Armstrong led a retired life because there was something wrong with him. One of the tales was that any excitement brought on an epileptic fit. One was that he was impotent; the child was adopted and not his, a story helped by the fact that I resembled neither of my parents. No proof was needed. It boiled down to the poisonous vagueness of "They say."

Then in the course of time, when the ground had been prepared, some carefully worded suggestions hit the movie magazines and the scandal sheets, phrased so there could be no libel suit. Nothing had to be proved. Just suggested. And the actor no longer got top billing, he began to get smaller parts and finally none at all and he couldn't find out why. That was when he started to drink. The family moved from a small house to a smaller apartment and at length my mother got a job clerking in a dress shop and my father was on the skids.

All this was reported to Natalie faithfully every week. And then the Hollywood representative informed Grace that the subject had left for New York. He had not had a drink in over a month and an old friend had lent him money to get a new start. An easy touch apparently, Grace said, and I saw my father wince.

"I've paid back every cent," he said.

Grace, whatever one thought of him, had done a painstaking job. He knew where my father lived and that he had a job coaching young actors. For this work he had used the name Burbage. He didn't seem able, even in such circumstances, to curb his impish humor.

Because he was under constant surveillance, one of Grace's staff had followed him to the General Post Office where he picked up my letter. Grace took up the trail, following him to Alcott. He called Natalie to report developments and then, when my father checked in at the rooming house, he had reported again.

"There was the hell of a storm that night," Grace said. "I had to spend it in my car because there are no motels in the district and I didn't want to be associated with the deal in any way. But when, in the morning, I heard about the murder I got uneasy. The room numbers weren't easy to make out in the dim light. So I went around to the morgue and the dead man was a stranger to me. I looked over his clothes and the stuff he'd had in his pocket and I'd already sneaked into his room and found this queer-looking gadget stuck on the blanket."

He held it out. It was a four-leaf clover in a plastic case. Natalie's lucky piece.

"Well, I had nothing to go on but a hunch, and I'm a believer in hunches. I called Mrs. Clifford and told her about the lucky piece. I could tell I had hit pay dirt. She knew I had the goods on her.

"So I wanted out. I don't like murder. She must have been half off her head to go out in a storm like that to kill a guy. And then she got the wrong one in the dark. So when I called, she gave me a check for twenty-five thousand, marked 'Paid in full.' "

"Blackmail" Fowler spoke for the first time.

Grace was not disturbed. "Oh, I'd earned my keep over the years. And I'd been busy on another line for her. About six to eight weeks ago I got instructions from Switzerland to check back on the record of her husband, John Clifford. She thought from something he said that he came from Boston. So I got in touch with a guy there. Clifford had apparently conned an elderly woman out of two hundred thousand and she had died a couple of weeks later, killed by a hit-run driver. I passed on the word, of course."

"So she suspected Clifford of wanting only her money," Fowler said. "That must have been a bitter blow to her pride."

Grace lighted a cigarette and blew out a cloud of smoke. "There's no getting around it. That woman had bad luck with her men. But when I heard this morning that Clifford had been stabbed to death just like the guy in the rooming house, I wanted out, like I said."

No one spoke for some time and then Grace said, "She was one of the most beautiful women I have ever seen, but there was something about her, like those vampires you read about—and I don't mean in the movies. She wanted—"

"Everything," Fowler said dully. "She wanted love and admiration; she wanted to be first. She had to have George Armstrong because he was the most glamorous man ever to come her way and when he, as she saw it, rejected her for Florence she saw it as a kind of betrayal. She couldn't be satisfied until she had destroyed them both. Her father had much the same quality. He was a violent man. Natalie's violence must have been—submerged. Netherfield hated Florence because she had taken the man who, in his opinion, belonged to Natalie. Only her mother loved Florence, loved her and rejoiced in her happiness, in her escape. I wonder now—" After a long time Fowler continued with an effort, "That accident of hers. Everyone assumed that Natalie suffered from a cramp and that her mother died saving her. I knew at the time, and her father knew, that Natalie had attempted to commit suicide. She could not endure rejection. But when her mother came to her aid, her mother who had wanted Florence to be happy—"

"No!" I cried.

"I hope not. We'll never know. And it doesn't matter any more." He turned to me. "You're so much like her. The same looks that would give any man a jolt. I would have expected her to be jealous instead of wanting to divide her whole estate with you."

"Personally," Tim said, his voice colorless, "I think Kate was just one more on the list. She must go the way her father and mother had gone. She got her here, disarmed her—"

"Last night," the doctor said, "she prepared a glass of milk with enough painkiller to make sure Miss Armstrong never woke up. She instructed Alice to give it to her."

I began to shake uncontrollably. It seemed as though the very ground had become unsure under my feet.

"I wonder," Grace asked, "whether Clifford really tried to bump her off on her honeymoon, the way her maid told her."

"I think," Fowler said, "that was pure malice on Alice's part. She didn't want anyone but herself to be close to Natalie."

"Armstrong, his wife, my Kate, Clifford—it's a big

score," Tim said. "A hell of a big score."

Fowler sighed. "A big score, yes. But where does the blame lie? Netherfield wanted his beautiful daughter to have all she wanted in life, taught her that she was entitled to it. But when she lost Armstrong, he decided to keep her an invalid, his very own property. And Alice with her jealous, obsessive love. And Natalie—" He paused. "Natalie, who wanted the world at her feet and was willing to bargain with God for what she wanted. And what she could not have she destroyed. Love, maybe? Possessiveness, maybe? God only knows. I'm willing to leave it to Him."

"What happens to me now?" Grace asked.

"You did your job and you got paid for it. Paid in full. Now get the hell out."

"Suits me," Grace said, and took his departure.

Night had fallen now and the cold was intensifying. The curious crowd dwindled away and the troopers got in their car and moved off.

Finally I said, thinking aloud, "When I went up, she said something odd. It sounded like, 'Put out the light,' but the light wasn't burning."

"To think of an actor whose daughter doesn't know Shakespeare!" my father exclaimed. "That's Othello when he says, 'Put out the light, and then put out the light' before he smothers Desdemona."

"She was going to write a poem," I said. "She was going to call it, 'Requiem for a Lost Love.' "

"She was a great poet," Fowler said, "and she left a great heritage of beauty. Perhaps that is all we have a right to expect of anyone."

Bates said, "Dinner is served."

212